RETURN OF THE DWARF KING

RETURN OF THE DWARF KING

THE ADVENTURES OF FINNEGAN DRAGONBENDER™
BOOK ONE

CHARLEY CASE   MARTHA CARR   MICHAEL ANDERLE

LMBPN Publishing
PMB 196, 2540 South Maryland Pkwy
Las Vegas, NV 89109

First US edition, December 2019
Version 1.01, February 2020
eBook ISBN: 978-1-64202-616-0
Print ISBN: 978-1-64202-617-7

CHAPTER ONE

"And another thing!" Finnegan Dragonbender proclaimed, leaning into the elf on the stool next to him. "The old organic ship *Earth* was far too big to truly be lost. She was unsinkable." He ran a hand through his thick brown hair, pulling it up to reveal the dwarven tattoos along the side of his head, then smoothed a few stray beard hairs before taking another sip of his drink.

"Unsinkable? I think the fact that it disappeared countermands that notion." The elf rolled his eyes, his lips twisted in mild annoyance.

"You heard me. Unsinkable. The historians have it all wrong."

The crowd at the bar was turning against him. Everyone liked a tale about the old days, but when someone started espousing their beliefs that the experts were wrong and only that one person knew the truth, people started to see them as a bit of a quack. And no one liked ducks at the bar. They made horrible drinking partners.

The difference was that Finn *knew* the *Earth* was still out there. He had recorded thousands of hours of television and radio signals that couldn't have come from anywhere but that ship. Of course, he didn't tell anyone about those. He wanted to be the one to find the old ship himself. And when he did, he was going to track down his hero. John Wayne.

Heads began to turn away, but Finn either didn't notice or didn't care. He just spoke louder so they could hear him.

"That ship was the crown jewel of the fleet in its day." He downed the rest of his brown liquor. "Had more people ridin' in lux...lugs... uh, comfort than anything like it since. Whole continents! And oceans for days. Beautiful."

Now everyone in the bar was doing their best not to make eye contact with the huge man. Finn had finally reached the "talk at you, not with you" stage of drunkenness. Either that, or he was just too stubborn to let the topic drop.

"And the cargo!" he shouted, slamming a fist down on the bar for emphasis. "The treasures that ship held! Even my distant cousin Fafnir was aboard with his whole workshop packed into storage."

"Fafnir?" Doubt clouded the elf's eyes. "The dwarven smith of legend, Fafnir? You're telling me that your cousin was a dwarf?" He looked Finn's six-foot-five frame up and down, shaking his head in disbelief.

"Hey." Finn leaned in and pointed at his eyes with two fingers. "My eyes are up here, bub. An' I take it you've never met a dwarf before. It's okay. We stay away from most people, seein' as they're all a bunch of pansies and such. Current company excluded," he added with a flourish of his hand at the rest of the people down the bar. "It's not your fault you weren't born dwarves, like me."

"Shut the fuck up, Finn. Always with the stupid *Earth* theories," a huge, gray-skinned troll a few stools down rumbled into his overly large mug.

Finn leaned into the bar, squinting to get a better look. "Winston? What are you doin' here? Tryn'a steal another artifact out from under me?"

"I hardly stole the last one." Winston's tone was far more refined than one would expect from such an ugly face. "I merely picked it up after you dropped it running from the locals. Maybe next time, you don't antagonize the entire population of a city while in the middle of a job, eh?"

"Maybe you should suck my—" *BEEELLLCCCHHH!* The burp was hard and loud, making the elf next to him scoot back in sudden fear of being vomited on.

"I'm sorry? What was that?" Winston pressed the lobe of his pointy ear closer to Finn. "I didn't quite catch that. Perhaps you would know how to hold your liquor better if you weren't as much an animal as that smelly lizard you call a friend."

Finn wiped the back of his hand across his mouth. "Now you've gone and done it. Penny don't stand for no backtalk."

A flash of blue and red streaked out of Finn's coat, darting down the bar. Glasses were either knocked to the floor or pulled out of the way just in time by quick hands as the scaly little creature made a beeline for the troll. Winston only raised an eyebrow and calmly took another drink.

The creature slid to a stop beside Winston's large, gray

3

hand, reared up on her hind legs, and unfolded her wings. There was a split second in which the bar fell silent as everyone took in Penny in all her small glory.

She was a foot and a half long from tail to tip, and most of that was in her long, serpentine neck and prehensile tail. Her body was barely larger than a fist and covered in metallic dark-blue scales, with a red stripe of small spikes down her back that ended with a spike on the tip of her tail. But it was her majestic butterfly wings that took the onlookers' breath away. They were each a foot wide and glowed iridescent blue in the dim light of the bar. She was a Faerie Dragon and a perfect example of her race.

Except that she was bonded to Finn, and he had taught her some nasty little tricks. Like how to breathe fire.

A white-hot jet of flame shot from the dragon's mouth and splashed across Winston's hand.

"Ow!" Winston shot to his feet, knocking his stool to the ground. With a quick flick of his hand, he sent Penny tumbling behind the bar with a squeak.

The crowd gasped and turned their heads to see what Finn would do.

"Why would you do that?" Finn yelled, diving over the bar to rescue his friend.

The crowd turned to Winston.

"Why would you have that little shit attack me?" he growled, holding the cool mug to his blistered hand. "You know trolls are susceptible to fire. You're out of control, Finn. How long have we been treasure hunters? Fifty years? In all that time, I have never once tried to harm you, at least not directly. That counts for something."

The crowd turned back as Finn popped up from behind

the bar, Penny on his shoulder, looking no worse for wear. Luckily, dragons were hard to hurt, even the small ones.

"What about Stalat Prime? You shot me in the arm!" He pulled up his sleeve, showing off the round scar.

The crowd turned back to Winston, whose face was a little greener as his green blood rushed to his cheeks in embarrassment. "That was a special circumstance. You were in disguise."

"I was dressed as a woman! You shot a woman!"

"Oh, please!" Winston threw his hands up in the air. "That was the worst disguise I have ever seen. I knew you weren't a woman."

"So, you admit you knew it was me!" Finn shouted, vaulting over the bar, his pant leg getting caught on a tap handle and making him crumple to the floor. He jumped back up to his feet and put a finger in Winston's face. "You also blew up the temple of Grax while I was still in it."

"Oh, damn," someone in the crowd murmured.

But he wasn't done.

"And I can't prove it," Finn's eyes turned from their normal dark brown to icy blue as he took another half step closer to the seven-foot troll, "but I'm pretty sure you were the one that took a shit in the ventilation shaft of my ship. You know how hard it is to get the smell of troll shit out of the air system?"

Winston smiled, showing off his yellow teeth. "I didn't think you would notice, with how bad that garbage heap you call a ship smells already."

"That's your problem, Winston." Finn leaned in. "You don't think."

Penny huffed a ring of smoke in the troll's face just to add injury to insult.

The crowd watched Winston and Finn staring each other down, realizing there was obviously a lot more than a barroom argument fueling that rage. There was history.

The first patron to turn and leave started a tidal wave of action as the bar cleared out in a matter of seconds. Even the bartender thought better of getting between the two hulking figures and slid through the door to the back room.

"You just can't seem to get that chip off your shoulder, can you, Dragonbender? What's the matter, you can't deal with the fact that you're the worthless third son of the dwarf king? Didn't get enough love from daddy? Is that it? Tossed out to make your own fortune to prove your worth?"

Winston's voice had dropped his civilized affectation and fallen back to what Finn thought of as the troll's true tone. Something like the sound of rocks being ground together.

"You know what me and Penny call you?" Finn said, a smile cracking his neatly trimmed beard. "We call you the Bottom Feeder. Always coming along to pick up our scraps. Why is it you don't go out and find your own artifacts? You too lazy to do some research on your own?"

Winston barked a laugh. "Me? You're the one who's obsessed with finding that old ship, *Earth*. That was so long ago, there's not going to be anything left. The original passengers would have died off eons ago. Even if it didn't crash into a star or get swallowed by a black hole, the engines would have broken down, and it would be a frozen ball of nothing by now, just floating through empty space. It's a pipe dream, Dragonbender. Just like your fantasy that you're actually worth something other than a good laugh.

"If I'm so bad at treasure hunting, then tell me, Dwarf King, why am I flying around in a state-of-the-art, hollowed-out moon while you're still trying to keep that piece-of-shit asteroid together with nothing but adhesive strips and your pathetic hopes and dreams?" Winston poked Finn in the forehead to drive the point home. "Maybe you should be happy your mother died early on in the war between our peoples. That way she didn't have to see what a piss-poor job she did raising you."

The smile dropped from Finn's face, and his eyes went nearly gray as power surged through his body. Winston recognized Finn's magical tell, but was too late to get out of the way. He only had enough time to make that stupid face someone makes right before they get hit by something they know is really going to hurt.

"*Gunna salainn!*"

A blast of white crystals shot from Finn's palm directly into Winston's chest, lifting the huge troll off his feet and sending him crashing into, and completely destroying, a table and three chairs. A cloud of white dust hung in the air where Winston had been, leaving a tang of salt in the mouth and nose. Penny sneezed, sending out a little jet of blue flame.

A moan rose from the floor, where Winston rolled back and forth, clutching his chest. Thick, green blood seeped out of the hundred or so wounds made by the rock salt Finn had blasted into his torso.

"Nobody talks bad about my momma." Finn spat salt

dust from his mouth in a phlegmy gob, then leaned over the troll's face. "I suggest you keep this little rivalry we have between *us* and leave our people out of it. We both know we don't belong back there, with their constant war and political backstabbing. But I'll make a deal with you. You don't say another word about my momma, and I won't kill you. Deal?"

"Deal," Winston groaned out.

Finn turned back to the bar. What little haze he had worked up over the hours of drinking had been burned off the instant his magic had flowed through him.

"Dammit, Winston. You know how hard it is for me to get my buzz on, with my dwarven blood. Now you've gone and made me waste all that time and effort." He spied the bartender peeking through the little window to the back room, and motioned for him to come out.

Finn had to give the guy credit for only hesitating a second before pushing the door open.

"Hey, listen." Finn leaned an elbow on the bar and put on his best apologetic face. "I can't believe this got so out of hand. What do I owe you for the drinks and the table?"

The bartender swallowed and looked up Finn's tab on the holographic ledger he wore around his wrist. "That'll be eighty-seven for the drinks, and, say, three hundred for the table and chairs?"

Finn sighed. It was almost all he had in his account, but he'd caused the damage, so he would pay to fix it. It was only right.

He swiped his wrist-wallet over the scanner in the bartop, and there was a mechanical *ding*, letting him know the payment had been taken.

"Wow. I really didn't think you were going to pay for that," the bartender said, leaning over the bar to take a look at the injured troll. "Is he going to be—oh shit!" The bartender's eyes went wide as he tried to push off the bar and get some cover from the troll.

Finn reacted automatically, knowing what the asshole behind him was up to. He reached under his coat and gripped the ornate handle that rested in the small of his back. With a practiced movement, he pulled on it and murmured the power word to activate it.

Ping!

The hypersonic round ricocheted off the flat of the axe blade that had materialized from the handle in Finn's hand. It was single-sided and swooped in a wicked flourish that ended in a razor-sharp hook. The flat of the blade glowed softly with dwarven runes.

"That was playing dirty, Winston." Finn pulled the axe blade from in front of the hyperventilating bartender's face and turned to the prone figure. "You know how me and Penny feel about playing dirty."

Winston still had one hand clutched to his chest, but the other gripped a pistol he had pulled from somewhere. The barrel was wavering in Finn's general direction, having missed his first shot and nearly taking out the only other person in the room. "You play dirty all the time, Dragonbender."

"Exactly." Finn moved faster than anyone his size had a right to and slammed the flat of the axe into Winston's surprised face.

There was a crunch and blood splattered from the troll's broken nose, splashing green across the beer-stained carpet. With a thump, Winston's head bounced once on the floor before lolling to the side, his lights thoroughly out.

Finn gave Winston one last look, then pulled out a cigar, bit off the tip, and spat it at him. "Don't worry too much about him," he told the barkeep. "He's a troll; he'll be back on his ugly feet in an hour or so. You might want to call Security, though. Pretty sure you can't have weapons on the station." He seemed to realize he was still holding his axe and quickly mumbled the power word.

The weapon began to fold in on itself in impossible ways until it disappeared completely, leaving only the ornate handle.

"Thanks for the drinks." He smiled and tipped an imaginary hat to the open-mouthed bartender. Then he turned and walked out the door with a casual wave over his shoulder.

Penny, on the other hand, nearly popped her shoulder out of its socket, she was waving with such enthusiasm.

Out on the main concourse of the space station, they turned and headed for their ship, the *Anthem*.

"You mind?" Finn presented the end of the cigar to Penny, who obliged him with a small flame that he greedily sucked into the rolled tobacco. Blowing out a plume of blueish-white smoke, he sighed in satisfaction. "Nothing like a good stogie after kicking some ass, eh, Penny?"

The little dragon stood on her hind legs, her claws digging in to keep her steady, and crossed her arms. The look she gave him was like a full-body eye roll.

"What? It was Winston. That jackass has been following us around for years. Plus, he shouldn't have said that about momma. That shit wasn't cool."

Penny at least agreed with him on the last part by giving a sharp nod. She pointed behind them and raised one of her eye ridges.

Finn turned in time to see several uniformed security personnel piling into the bar. One of them spotted Finn, and pointed, shouting to his comrades. Two of them took off at a run in Finn's direction.

"I think that just about wraps up our stay here." He turned and ran full speed for his docking port, the cigar still in his mouth and puffing like a locomotive.

Penny hung on as best she could, but after a few jostling steps, she leapt off his shoulder and took flight, easily keeping pace with him.

Finn had to dodge his way around cargo containers and lines of passengers to make his way. He jumped over a row of benches, scaring a halfling who happened to be lying on one of said benches, trying to catch a little sleep before his connecting flight. When the poor guy sat up to yell at Finn, his head clipped the foot of the security guard coming in hot on Finn's tail. The two of them tumbled to the ground in a heap, making the second guard go around the benches.

That gave Finn enough time to swipe his wrist over the ID pad and unlock the door to his ship's berth. He slipped into the airlock and pulled the door closed just as the second security guard got close.

Smacking the big red button on the wall, Finn started the airlock procedure, and atmosphere began to fill the small space to equalize the *Anthem* to the station. The guard pounded on the glass, but Finn just waved and stepped onto his ship, closing the door behind him once Penny was through.

"Let's go find us some treasure, Penny. The cupboards are looking a little thin right now." Finn glanced at the account balance on his wrist display and grimaced. "Some cheap treasure."

CHAPTER TWO

Penny swooped down into the maintenance well, landing on Finn's shoulder.

"Cheep, cher peep!" She flapped her iridescent wings excitedly, interrupting his grunting efforts to loosen a bolt with an oversized wrench with a few quick jets of flame and a ladylike chirp.

"Come on, Penny, I'm a little busy here. Just tell me." Finn wiped sweat from his brow and pulled on the wrench for all he was worth. When that didn't work, he planted a foot on the bulkhead and added his leg to the pulling fest. All at once, the bolt let loose, throwing off Finn's balance and sending him to the deck, ass first.

Penny fluttered down onto his lap, her insistent mood not deterred in the least. She pointed out the top of the well to the main cabin. "Squee. Click click, squee!" she stomped a foot on his knee for emphasis.

"Okay, okay. Let me just bolt on the refurbished temp modulator. You may be fine with the heat and humidity, but my dwarven bones can't take it anymore. It's got to be

13

two hundred degrees in here." He mopped his brow with an already soaked handkerchief and stuffed it back into the pocket of his greasy maintenance suit.

Penny didn't like waiting, but she let him replace the unit since the old one was already off, and she knew he was useless when it got too hot. But she still tapped her foot impatiently.

"The tapping isn't helping. But you could hand me the other two bolts if it's not too much of an inconvenience, Your Highness."

Penny narrowed her eyes, but grabbed a bolt in each hand and flew them over to Finn's waiting glove.

"Thanks."

Penny went back to tapping, this time at double tempo, with her arms crossed.

Finn knew better than to comment and just worked faster.

After attaching the 'refurbished' unit (it was actually just the old one, which had been going out intermittently before Finn had replaced it with the current one), he switched the power on and sighed in relief when the air vents started pumping out cool air once again.

The unit flickered and went out, shutting off the cool air, along with its indicator light.

Finn growled and hit the bulkhead Fonzie-style, sending the unit into flickering fits before it powered up once again.

"All right." He pulled himself out of the maintenance access and slid the floor panel closed. "What's so important that you needed me to come see?"

"Squeech click."

"A signal? So what? We get random signals all the time." Despite his naysaying, Finn was making his way to the bridge.

The *Anthem* had seen better days. Old parts no better than scrap littered the workbenches. Only about half the lights still worked, casting a gloomy feel over much of the ship, and the ones that did still work flickered randomly.

Finn hated to admit it, but the old girl was on her last journey if he couldn't find the parts to overhaul her real soon.

A static-filled transmission came out of the speakers on the bridge. Finn cocked his head and listened. There was something familiar about the pattern, but he couldn't place it.

"Does the readout give us a clue who it is?" He sat down at the navigator's station and began to scroll through the data associated with the rhythmic sound. "There's nothing here. It's like whoever's sending the signal didn't know how..." Finn sat up straighter, a faraway look on his face. "Wait. I know that pattern."

"Squee!" Penny was jumping in circles with excitement. She knew exactly what it was, but she wanted him to figure it out on his own.

"That's the sound of an Organicum Industria Core engine." Finn's wide eyes made Penny do a backflip and shoot a jet of flame into the air. "Those are the same engines used in the terrestrial class super cruisers. The only way we could pick up this signal would be if one of those ships was running, and all five of the others are either out of range or decommissioned. That leaves one ship in the entire universe that could possibly be using those engines." Finn scooped Penny up and held her in front of his face, their combined excitement making the two of them nearly vibrate. "We found the *Earth*!"

"Click scree!"

"Oh, man. You said it. Have you been able to pinpoint the location?"

Penny gave a toothy grin and a nod.

Finn tossed her into the air with a "Whoo!" letting her catch herself with her wings as he jumped into the pilot's seat. "Put in the coordinates, Penny. We're going to go find us a relic of history."

Penny fluttered down to the navigation controls and started inputting numbers. She gave a complicated series of squeaks, clicks, and grunts as she worked, casting a wary eye Finn's way every once in a while.

"It'll be fine. I know the old girl's on her last legs, but she's got at least one more good jump in her. Besides, we need to get the parts to fix her, and there should be plenty of them on *Earth* if the history books are correct. Even if we go to the closest station, we can't afford to buy what we'd need to take off again. This is our last chance."

Penny frowned but gave a squeak of acceptance and hit the enter button.

Finn smiled over his shoulder. "Don't worry, we'll be fine. I promise."

After a second's consideration, he buckled the five-point harness and tightened the straps.

"Squee?"

Finn shrugged. "Better safe than sorry."

Penny gave him the stink-eye but crawled inside his jacket and reached a clawed hand out to zip it shut. There was a muffled "Krick," and Finn felt her tap his chest to indicate she was ready.

"Really? You're not even going to stick your head out? Don't you want to see this thing when we get there?"

After another second's hesitation, a claw poked out the collar of his jacket and zipped it open just enough for her to slip her scaly blue head out.

"Right. Let's do it."

Finn hit the warp button.

The *Anthem* shook and shimmied. Loud tearing sounds echoed from below the deck plates, and the lights flickered even more wildly than normal. The controls were dead in Finn's hands, along with the whole bank of sensors.

"Shit! We've lost everything. Penny, get in there and see what you can do." Finn opened the small hatch they had cut into the side of the flight console and secured with adhesive strips.

Penny darted into the hole. After only a few seconds, she let out a triumphant squeak, and the main viewscreen lit up.

Finn pumped a fist. "All right! Wait. Something's wrong with the image. It's all orange and flickery."

Penny stuck her head out of the hole. "Squee, click scree?"

Finn looked at her, then back at the screen, his eyes going wide. "Oh, shit. You're right. We're in atmosphere. I need the throttle control, at the very least. And fast."

"Eep!"

Penny darted back into the console. Random banging and scraping noises emanated from the hardware, followed by a jet of flame and a small puff of smoke.

The ship was shaking even more violently now that they were getting into the really thick atmosphere and still hadn't hit the brakes. The flames in the viewscreen had turned from orange to white, and the interior of the asteroid ship was beginning to grow warm despite the new temp unit. A loud bang and a clatter told Finn that things were starting to fall off the workbenches.

"Anytime, Penny." Finn gritted his teeth and tried the reverse throttle once again. Nothing. "Actually, I take that back. Now would be better than anytime."

An angry series of clicks followed by a steady jet of flame from Penny told him she was working her tail off and not to interrupt.

The scanner flickered to life and drew Finn's attention. Apparently they had warped in just a little too close to the surface, and had been caught in *Earth*'s gravity well. They were coming in hot right in the center of a medium-sized continent. It looked like they would land at the edge of a mountain range.

Unless Penny didn't fix the damn throttle—then they would *impact* on the edge of a mountain range. The altitude numbers, coupled with the speed numbers, were not painting a pretty picture for the *Anthem* and her two passengers.

"SCREE!"

Penny shot out of the hole and started hitting switches to reset the controls. Finn joined her, speeding up the process by a few seconds. Flipping the last switch, Penny unfolded her wings and dove across the console to wrap herself around the throttle control and jerk it back as far as it would go.

Finn was slammed into his five-point harness, the air forced from his lungs. He didn't know if they had braked early enough, but he did know he needed to get hold of Penny before they touched down. This was going to be a rough landing all the way around.

He was able to pry her from the throttle, but a glance at the scanner told him there was no time to secure her properly. Instead, he clutched her to his chest as tight as he could, hoping it would be enough.

A great rending sound came from the guts of the ship, and Finn was thrown sideways in the restraints as the ship clipped the edge of a stone outcropping. The viewscreen had finally started showing something other than white-hot flames, but ridges full of trees and stone were not a much better sight.

Finn tried to steer as best he could with one hand, but the controls were sluggish. He was able to tilt the ship just enough to miss the outcropping in front of them, so they just ricocheted off the stone instead of cracking open like an egg. He aimed them toward a lush, green valley at the bottom of the mountain they were practically skidding down.

They were jolted once again as the asteroid ship bounced once, sending splintered trees and hunks of earth and stone into the air. They hit again, this time sliding a little longer before the ground fell away in a cliff, letting the *Anthem* sail another quarter mile before it finally plunged into the soft soil of the valley below, sending up a rooster tail of dirt and vegetation.

Finn still held onto Penny, his hands sweaty, and his breath coming in ragged gulps. The harness had done its job, but it was going to leave some bruises, and he might have broken a rib.

He released Penny, who wobbled a little before plopping down and shaking her head. Hitting the release button, Finn shimmied out of the harness and promptly fell out of the pilot's chair. It took him a second or two to understand that the ship was sitting at an extreme angle and it wasn't him that was leaning over too far.

"Well. That could have been worse." Finn shook his head, pulling himself to his feet while keeping a hand on the pilot's chair for support.

The *Anthem* groaned as it settled and pinged metallically as it cooled from re-entry.

"Let's see what's left of the old girl, and set up the cloaking crystals before the locals come to investigate."

Penny gave a trill and took a few wobbly steps before giving him a thumbs-up and falling off the console. She bobbed up on flapping wings before hitting the tilted deck and heading toward the maintenance closet.

CHAPTER THREE

"Most of this, we can repair."

Finn "sat" on the wall and leaned back on the deck plates. Penny was on his knee, looking over the list he had written out on an old slip of paper.

"I would like to replace it all, but worst-case scenario, I think we can get the *Anthem* limping along with repairs. However, the warp drive and the main controller circuit are toast and need to be replaced."

"Squee. Cheep skee cheep," Penny said, accompanied by a small puff of smoke.

Finn rolled his eyes. "I know the rest needs replacing eventually. I'm just saying that at minimum, we can repair. The cargo holds on *Earth* were stocked pretty well, but I'm afraid that over the years, most of those parts have been used. I'm just keeping it real. Besides, if we can snatch a few artifacts before we go, we will be able to afford a retrofit of what we need at the closest station."

Finn rolled to his feet, one hand on the deck to keep himself steady.

"Come on, we need to get to that city we saw coming in. That will be the best place to start. Maybe we'll get lucky and find a Huldu right off. Those guys like to make trades, and I'm sure we have something in the hold that would interest them."

Penny fluttered into the air and gave him a look that said he was dreaming. "Squeek?"

Finn picked his way to his room and pulled himself through the door, and onto the wall of the small compartment. "They could be there. Just because they worked in the engine rooms doesn't mean they don't come out sometimes. It's not like they need to be doing a lot of flying if our readings were right. This ship hasn't done anything but orbit this star for a while. I'm sure they've incorporated themselves into society by now."

Finn was able to climb his dresser and bed to reach his closet. He quickly changed into his adventuring gear: a black shirt and pants, and the harness he kept all his tools in. The brown leather harness ran over his shoulders and chest and had two straps that looped through his belt. It held the haft of Fragar, his dwarven-made axe, in a holster at the small of his back, and several healing potions in molded leather pockets on the straps. He pulled his jacket back on and jumped off the bed, then slid out the door.

Penny followed him to the airlock—a process that took a good twenty minutes, with the ship half on its side—and climbed in with him. He hit the button, and the inner door closed, then the pressure equalized with the outside atmosphere, and the outer door slid open.

The smell of fresh air billowed into the small space, making Finn smile.

"It's been a while since we weren't breathing recycled farts, eh, Penny?" He took a deep breath through his nose, savoring the smell of fresh-turned soil and pine.

The opening was half-covered with dirt, but Finn was able to crawl out across the still-warm soil. Once he was far enough from the curving rocky surface of the *Anthem*, he stood and walked a few dozen yards, then turned to see the damage.

The asteroid the ship was made from was buried nearly halfway into the soft earth. Steam and smoke wafted into the still night sky, thinning out and dissipating as the air above the sheltered valley stirred it into thin clouds.

The ship itself was still in one piece, and he didn't see any cracks that shouldn't be there. It took him a good ten minutes to walk the perimeter, see the ship from every angle, and to make sure the cloaking rods had been properly placed by Penny.

Not that he thought she had done it wrong, but it was always better to double-check.

"Were you able to cover the plowed-up ground behind the ship as well? Wouldn't want someone to see that. It just ends where the illusion ends."

"Chirp chee," Penny said indignantly.

"Hey, I'm just thinking about that time on Reint Prime." Finn raised an eyebrow at her fluttering blue form. "If I recall correctly, it was you who forgot about the scorch marks our landing jets left across that field. Nearly got us killed."

Penny huffed, but she wouldn't meet his eyes as she said, "Screip chip chee."

"I know you're sorry, I wasn't trying to make you feel

bad. I was just checking." He smoothed his beard, taking a good look around at his surroundings for the first time. "It's not like you don't save my ass all the time," he mumbled to himself, but the grin on Penny's face told him that she had heard.

They were in a lush mountain valley; there didn't seem to be any buildings or roads in sight. The trees were green and thick, despite the chill in the air, and a small river or large stream ran the length of the valley, making bubbling and splashing noises in the background. Turning to the east, he could see the lights of a large city blotting out the stars.

"Looks like we go that way. I'm guessing it's at least ten miles." He pointed at the glowing sky beyond where the water was flowing.

Penny swooped down and landed on his shoulder.

They looked at one another for a second before Finn grinned like a child. "I can't believe we actually found it. This is going to be amazing. Think of the treasures we'll find. We could finish your horde if we're lucky."

Penny grinned and blew a ring of smoke from one nostril in excited agreement.

An hour later, Finn crested the downhill ridge of the valley and saw the city sprawled before them. Lights spread out as far as the eye could see, glowing a dim orange in the night.

He blinked a few times, taking it all in. "This is insane. It just goes on forever. Where are the towers?"

Every city Finn had ever been to throughout the galaxy had used magic to erect huge towers that could hold millions of people. It was the most efficient way for so many people to live in one place, but this was madness.

"Why would they spread out like this? It must take forever to get anywhere."

Penny huffed in agreement.

They had seen some shit during their travels, but this was in the top three of weirdest places, easy.

Finn started down the hill, using the odd tree to keep himself from sliding. "Maybe there's a magical dead spot here, or the towers were trying to pull too much energy or something."

"Cherp, shir." Penny rolled her eyes, fluttering between branches beside him.

"I don't know why they would build on a dead spot. It was just a guess," he grunted as he slid a few feet before catching himself on a sapling that bent over alarmingly against his weight.

Being a dwarf, Finn was able to see just fine, even without a moon in the sky, so when he almost fell off a cliff, where the slope he was descending suddenly ended, his surprise made his heart jump up into his throat.

He grabbed the trunk of a tree on the cliff's edge and was able to stop himself from stepping off into nothing. Penny came shooting around him and slammed into his chest, trying with all her might to push him back from the edge.

The tiny dragon had no effect on Finn's balance, but he appreciated the gesture.

Getting both feet back on solid ground, he looked left, then right along the cliff's edge.

"This is going to take forever." Finn blew out a long breath.

The city's edge was not far—at least, not for Penny, but Penny could fly. Finn, however, saw about a thousand obstacles he would need to traverse before he even got close.

"Tell you what. I'm going to head this way," Finn pointed to the left, "and you fly ahead to see if you can find a trail or something. There has to be a way down this mountain."

Penny gave him a nod and took off, rising above the tree cover before moving in the direction indicated. Finn watched her go, hoping she would be able to find an alternative route before too long. He liked the outdoors, but heights were not a dwarf's favorite thing.

Finn kept an eye on the cliff and moved carefully after the faerie dragon. He would have moved further into the forest, but he wanted to stay in plain sight so Penny would have no trouble spotting him, so instead, he made slow progress, his heart beating just a little faster than usual.

Finn had to stop and marvel at how well the great ship *Earth* had held up over the eons. Usually, ecosystems fell apart over a long enough timeline, but here, it seemed like the selected plants and animals had flourished. He wondered if it had to do with the particular star the ship now orbited, or if it was a product of careful curation by the Huldu.

Continuing on, Finn saw a light moving through the trees

about a half-mile in front of him, and he instinctively ducked down beside a thick pine, using the dense needles for cover. Though, if whatever he was hiding from could pick him out this far away, then it was too late to hide. But years of training in infiltration kept him crouched. The second he underestimated a guard or priestess would be the second he got caught.

The light bobbed and flickered, turning corners and disappearing, then turning back as whatever it was followed the curve of the mountain in an upward direction. It was making slow progress, but it was consistent, and Finn quickly understood it was a vehicle of some kind. Probably one of the fancy, Magic-propelled carriages that were popular back when *Earth* had first taken off. Then he remembered the films he had recorded and watched from *Earth*, and he smiled. No, the light was coming from a car. He remembered the round, bulbous vehicles from the John Wayne films he so loved.

Finn stood and picked up the pace. He wanted to see one of these Fords for himself.

He was no more than a hundred yards further along when Penny swooped down through the trees and landed on his shoulder.

"Cher shriip. Chee chi." She was excited, and her little jet of flame could have blinded Finn, but luckily, he knew what happened when she got excited and had closed his eyes to preserve his dark vision.

"I know. I saw it just a few minutes ago." Finn started jogging. "I wonder if we can catch a ride down into the city."

Penny made another series of chirps and squeaks,

careful to keep her enthusiasm down and not jet flame in his face.

Finn was disappointed to hear that the vehicle was moving too fast to catch on foot, but he brightened when she said there was a second one coming from the other direction, and if he hurried, he should be able to catch it.

Finn ducked a little further into the woods to keep away from the cliff's edge and started running. His long legs ate up the distance. Dwarves weren't fast runners, being quicker off the line with explosive movements like an alligator, but they were hardy, and once they set a pace, they could keep it up over very long distances.

Crashing through the underbrush and low-hanging branches, Finn made very good time. After about five minutes of hard running, he glimpsed lights shining through the trees. They weaved and bounced as the vehicle drove along the dirt road Penny had told him was there.

Finn was afraid he was going to miss the oncoming vehicle and picked up speed, his breath becoming labored. The lights were getting closer, and he judged he would make it to the road just as the lights did. It was going to be close.

Penny had taken wing as soon as he started crashing through tree branches instead of ducking around them. Finn wished he had her ability to cover ground so fast, but wishing never got anyone anywhere, so instead, he focused on his legs pumping up and down, his eyes down so he wouldn't trip on an unseen root or stone.

He was still paying attention to the ground when the trees suddenly gave way, and he found himself sliding to a stop on a hard-packed gravel road, two headlights coming directly at him. The sound of tires locking up and plowing furrows in the dirt and tossing rocks his way made Finn throw a hand up, but it was too little too late.

Finn felt the air forced out of his lungs as a large, metal grille hit him in the chest. It sent him flying to land on his back and he slid down the road about twenty feet, kicking up dust the whole way.

He blinked a few times, staring into the night sky, his ears ringing and his chest throbbing from the impact. A cloud of dust from the vehicle wafted over him, backlit by the headlights.

"What in the actual fuck!" a man's voice shouted, followed by a door slamming. He had a bit of an accent that made him enunciate the "u" in "fuck" extra hard.

Finn sat up, rubbing his chest and checking to make sure there wasn't any permanent damage.

"Sorry about that, friend," he called to the silhouette of the man jogging toward him.

With a little effort, Finn got to his feet as the man slid to a stop beside him. Finn stood a good foot taller than him, and was easily twice as wide. He gave the man a toothy smile.

For the driver's part, he immediately took a step back from the giant he had just hit with his truck and didn't seem to have hurt at all.

"Whoa. You are a man, right? Not, like, a grizzly in clothes?"

"Actually, I'm a dwarf, Peabrain. Finnegan Dragonbender." Finn held out a meaty hand for the man to shake.

"I'm pretty sure you aren't allowed to say that. I think they prefer 'little people,'" he said with a shaky voice, but after a second, he shook Finn's offered hand. "You all right, buddy? You came out of nowhere!"

Finn had no idea what he meant by 'little people,' but he let it go. The man was obviously traumatized by the accident and not in his right mind.

"I was trying to catch you," Finn said, and the man paled slightly. Finn clarified, "I need a ride into town. My...transportation broke down, and I need to find some parts. Perhaps you know where I might find a Huldu?"

"Man, I don't know where you're from, but I believe they are called Hindus. I think there's a Hindu church in Lakewood, but I can't remember for sure." He took a second to look Finn over. "If you want, I can drop you off at the Kum & Go right off 70. I'm sure you can get a tow truck or something. You'll have to ride in my truck bed since I have my dogs in the front."

Finn smiled. "A ride would be wonderful. Thank you, Peabrain."

"Look, I know I hit you with my truck, but you don't need to keep calling me names, man. You can just call me Joe."

"Joe. Thanks for the ride," Finn said, walking back to the truck.

"Just don't sue me, bro," Joe mumbled, opening the driver door to his jacked-up truck.

Finn's eyes widened when he was past the headlights and able to see the truck for the first time. It was nothing like the rounded, small things from the John Wayne movies he was used to.

It must be from a different manufacturer, Finn reasoned.

Putting a hand on the edge of the bed right around chest level, he pulled and jumped, launching himself into the steel bed of the silver truck in one leap.

"Goddamn!" Joe exclaimed, his eyes wide. "You're a strong motherfucker."

"It's all part of being a dwarf," Finn said jovially, settling down in the bed and smiling.

"You can't *say* that, dude," Joe mumbled, climbing into the driver's seat and closing the door.

The tires spun a little before gaining traction, and then they slowly started down the mountain road.

Penny swooped down, having watched the whole interaction from the air. She settled on Finn's knee and narrowed her eyes.

"What?" Finn asked, his smile not fading in the least.

Penny began chirping her theory.

After a few turns in the road, Finn held up a hand to stop her long-winded explanation. "I know it's going to be a little different than the other places we've been. I mean, this ship's been out here for a long time without any supply runs, so they would have had to adapt, but they're still Peabrains. Once we get into the city, you'll see. It'll be no time until we find a Huldu."

Penny kept her mouth shut, but she gave him an "I hope you're right" look.

CHAPTER FOUR

D r. Mila Winters tiredly climbed out of her black
Hellcat Challenger and slid her credit card into the
gas pump's reader. She selected the premium option, and
after inserting the nozzle into the tank, she locked the
handle in the on position and leaned against the car's back
fender, pulling out her phone.

As she opened her email, two large moths landed on the
shoulder of her black leather jacket. They flexed their
wings and settled down as if her shoulder were the most
comfortable place in the world.

This was not an uncommon occurrence for Mila. Since
she was a little girl, bugs of all kinds seemed to flock to her.
When she was young, it had really freaked her out, but
over the years, she'd become used to it, even enjoying the
little interactions. She had never come across a bug that
wasn't respectful, and she tried to show them respect in
return.

"Hello, there. How's your night going, ladies?" Mila
smiled at the two on her shoulder. She never understood

how she knew if a bug was male or female, she just did. "Hopefully, it's going better than mine. I feel like it's nothing but work, work, work lately. Not to mention my coworker Jeff just up and disappeared. Yeah! Disappeared. He left me all his Viking bullshit to translate while he's supposedly on sabbatical. Can you believe that?"

The moths cocked their heads at her.

"Yeah, I'm not sure I believe it either."

The two moths bobbed a few times and took off again, circling the overhead light before heading into the night to find themselves a couple of strapping young men.

Mila laughed. That wasn't the first time she had talked to a bug that had stopped to check her out, but it was the first time she'd ever complained to one about work. She was getting a little delirious from exhaustion.

She had just spent the last twelve hours at Dinosaur Ridge, inspecting and cataloging a suspected ancient Native American campsite. The work would be ongoing since she'd been able to find several indications that the site was legitimate. It was good for science, but not so good for her weekend. The amount of paperwork she was going to have to file was daunting, and she was already backlogged, with the last shipment of Jeff's Viking relics sitting in her workshop at the museum. She was trying to decide if she would work on it over the weekend, or if she would wait until Monday and just embrace the fact that she was going to be behind for a few weeks.

She was halfway through another email from her boss at the Denver Museum of Nature and Science, where she was the lead anthropologist, when a jacked-up Chevy truck pulled into the gas station and stopped at the convenience store's front door.

Normally, the sight of a truck with a twelve-inch lift wouldn't make her bat an eye, not in Denver, but this truck had one of the largest men she had ever seen in her life riding in the back. He was quite handsome, and his exquisitely trimmed black beard and hair were not uncommon sights in the hip, urban areas of the city. However, the symbols tattooed along the sides of his head, where the hair was clipped short under the neck-length hair on top, caught her eyes.

She wouldn't have thought anything of the symbols, except that she had been working with several artifacts that had some of the same markings on them. They were runes, and from the quick glance she got of them, they were perfectly formed.

The pet lizard riding on his shoulder was a bit odd as well, but then again, this was Denver. If she didn't know any better, though, she would say it was a tiny dragon with its wings folded back.

The bearded man stood and hopped out of the truck bed, barely flexing his legs when he landed from the five-foot drop. He gave the bed a few slaps and the truck took off, barking the tires in its haste to get out of there. The large man looked around as if he had never seen a gas station before, and when he turned her way, a huge smile split his neat black beard and he waved.

Mila blushed and quickly looked behind her to see if there was someone else, but she was the only one at the pumps. Considering it was eleven-thirty at night on a Wednesday, that wasn't unusual. When she looked back, he had opened the door to the convenience store. She could swear that before the door closed behind him, his pet lizard had given her a wave as well.

She blinked a few times, then rubbed her eyes. She must be more tired than she thought.

"Why is it that all the handsome guys have weird shit like pet lizards? Can't you just get a dog like a normal person?"

The pump clicked, making her jump, and she replaced the nozzle. Ripping the receipt free, she fell into the driver's seat and raised her phone to finish reading the email from her boss. She got to the end and realized she hadn't comprehended a single word. Instead, she was thinking about the big guy's rune tattoos. The more she thought about it, the more she would have sworn that the tattoos had been glowing faintly.

"What are the odds that I'm trying to translate a bunch of runes, and a guy with rune tattoos is literally dropped off in front of me?"

Mila frowned, put her phone in the cupholder, and pressed the button to start the Hellcat. The engine roared to life, then settled down to a rumbling purr. She didn't put the car in drive, however. Instead, she waited for the guy to come back out, just to be sure she wasn't seeing things.

Thinking of all the artifacts back in her workshop, her head began to swim. There was just so much work to do, and she was absolute crap when it came to rune translation. The whole push for her to take on the Viking finds was from her boss, who thought Viking lore was "sexy" and would get more people into the museum.

He was probably right. Everybody liked a good Viking

story, but Mila specialized in Native American and South American cultures, so switching to rune translation was a learning curve for her.

None of this would have been a problem if Jeff hadn't suddenly up and left. They had worked across the hall from one another for the last three years, and she thought they were at least friendly, but he hadn't said a thing to her before dumping his whole workload in her lap and taking off. He did leave a note, but it was in that damned runic script he loved. She had tried for two days to translate it but had gotten nowhere. When she asked their boss where Jeff had gone, all he would tell her was that he was on sabbatical, and would be gone for the foreseeable future.

None of it sat right with Mila, but she didn't really have a reason to believe anything different. Except for the note he had left her, which she couldn't even read.

The guy's tattoos gave her an idea. She wasn't sure if it was a good idea, or if she was just too tired to understand how bad an idea it was, but she was going to give it a try.

Pulling up the photo gallery app on her phone, she started scrolling through pictures until she found the one she was looking for. She'd had made a scan of Jeff's note and was planning to post it to Reddit to see if anyone could translate it for her. She didn't really want to do that, just in case it was personal, but so far, nothing else had worked. Maybe this guy could help. He did seem to at least understand runes, or his tattoos wouldn't be so perfect.

It was a long shot, but at this point, she didn't have anything to lose.

Pressing the ignition button again, she shut the engine off and climbed back out of the car. Before she could change her mind, she marched toward the convenience store, her phone in hand.

"What's the worst that could happen?" she reasoned when she was about ten feet from the door.

A blue flash of light from inside the store made her stop in her tracks. A second later, a young man in the store's uniform slammed the door open and sprinted out and around the building. He was gone before she could say anything, and when she turned back to the door, the large bearded man was pushing his way out, his face full of confusion.

"Hey! Stop! I just wanted to trade for some information!" the man shouted, throwing his hands up, and disturbing his pet lizard.

The lizard lost its balance and, to Mila's horror, unfurled two, foot-wide butterfly style wings to steady itself, before folding them back and settling on the man's shoulder once again.

Mila's mouth hung open, her hand outstretched, holding her phone, as she began to take a step back.

The man glanced her way and leaned in to take a look at the small screen. Then a huge smile spread across his face.

"Finally!" he said, his eyes locking with hers. "Someone who still knows the script!" He frowned, reading further. "However, I have to say this is a pretty dour letter to show a stranger." His smile returned slightly. "Are you a dryad?"

A whole lot of information was fighting to be heard first in Mila's mind; the thing on his shoulder that was definitely some kind of dragon, the fact that this guy could obviously read Jeff's note, the store clerk running off into the night, just how big this guy was, the fact that they were now alone and he out-sized her by at least a factor of three, the blue flash of light that was not in any way natural.

But the thing that won out over all of that other stuff was his last statement.

"A dryad?" she asked, blinking dumbly.

His face fell a little. "Oh, sorry. I see now that your teeth aren't sharp. That was my bad." He held out a huge hand. "My name is Finnegan Dragonbender. It's a pleasure to meet you...?"

She didn't know why she did it. She should have turned and run, but instead, she reached out with her free hand and shook his. "Mila Winters."

"Mila, that's a good name. Sounds almost elvish." He hiked a thumb to his shoulder. "This is Penny. She's glad to meet you too."

Penny rolled her eyes and snorted a small flame from her nostrils.

That little jet of flame was what put Mila over the edge. It was too much.

Her mind shut down. The world went black, and she fainted.

CHAPTER FIVE

Finn quickly reached out and scooped up the short black-haired woman before she could hit the ground. He had seen the wild look in her eyes and figured she was about to run like the store clerk, so he was a little surprised when she'd fainted instead.

He looked down at her, cradled in his arms, appreciating her fine features and olive skin. A warm feeling spread through him, and he glanced up at Penny, who craned over his shoulder to get a good look at the small woman.

"You know, Penny..." Finn gave her an earnest look. "I'm starting to think magic isn't really a thing here on *Earth*."

Penny rolled her eyes and locked gazes with him. "Squeeeee?" she drew out sarcastically.

"Yeah, all right. Enough attitude. It was your shooting flames into the night that finally pushed her over the edge."

Finn looked around the empty gas station, not wanting

to have to answer any questions about why he was holding an unconscious woman. That sort of thing didn't go over well on any planet.

"Is that black vehicle hers?" Finn asked Penny, jutting his chin at the Hellcat.

Penny shrugged, then hopped off Finn's shoulder and onto the woman's stomach. With careful hands, she began searching the pockets of her jeans. After a few seconds, she pulled out a red key fob with a few metal house keys, attached by a frog keychain.

Penny pressed a button, and the lights on the Hellcat flashed. She pressed another button, and they flashed twice.

"I guess that's hers." Finn started for the car. "Hey, Penny, grab her screen device thing. She dropped it."

Penny swooped off his shoulder and grabbed her phone from the ground, the bulk of it making her flight unstable.

Finn awkwardly opened the door of the car and gently set the woman in the driver's seat, closing the door after her. Then he walked to the other side of the car, opened the passenger door, and climbed in, but left the door open.

Penny came around the open door, flying low, the weight of the phone keeping her down. Her teeth were gritted in effort. Finn reached for it, and Penny gratefully released the heavy thing and landed on his lap to take a quick breather.

Finn looked at the woman, making sure she was doing okay, then read the note again.

"Penny, take a look at this." Finn held the phone screen out so Penny could get a look at it from her perch on his knee. "Does it seem like it was written by a dwarf?"

Penny scanned the note and shrugged. After a second's more consideration, she shook her head. "Squee scritt?" she suggested.

Finn frowned and looked back at the screen. "Yeah, I was thinking troll too. I thought we didn't find any trolls on the manifest."

Penny again shrugged, "Clich sri cree."

"True, it wasn't an official manifest, but we paid good money for that thing."

Penny raised an eye ridge and puffed some smoke out of the sides of her mouth.

Finn waved her comment off. "Just because it was wrong about a few things doesn't mean it was fake. Maybe it was just an early copy or something."

This time, Penny rolled her eyes, but before she could comment, her head snapped to the side to look at the woman in the driver's seat.

Finn turned and saw that she was awake. "Oh, hello. Sorry, we didn't know where else to put you. Hope you don't mind, but it seemed like your friend was in trouble," Finn held up the phone and shook it, "so I thought I'd better stick around. Plus, Penny is really sorry for the scare she gave you earlier."

Penny smiled, showing rows of sharp, white teeth against her blue skin. Finn knew she was trying to be friendly, but he also knew that seeing a smiling dragon was a mixed bag for the recipient.

The woman tensed when she saw Penny baring her teeth at her and slowly reached down between her seat and the door. She never took her eyes off the dragon, and Penny, for her part, glanced Finn's way while trying to hold the smile, which was quickly slipping from genuine to forced.

In a sudden move that made both Finn and Penny jump, the small woman pulled a short bat from beside her seat and brandished it at them in the confined space.

"Who the fuck are you?" Her voice was high and tight with mania, but it also had a musical quality that Finn really liked. "Why are we in my car? What the fuck is that thing?" The last was said with a shaky finger pointed at Penny. "Is it a dragon?"

Penny's smile grew and she began nodding. "Squee. Click shii!" A small jet of flame punctuated the statement, making the woman jump back against the door and point the end of the bat at her again.

"Whoa, let's all just calm down here," Finn said, holding up his hands.

The end of the bat swung to point at Finn's face. "Don't you tell me to calm down, Mountain Man! You tell me what the fuck is going on right now, or I will beat you both to bloody pulps."

"Um, okay." Finn carefully smoothed down his beard, then held out the phone for her to take.

She snatched it out of his hands and looked at the note on the screen. Her demeanor changed instantly, as if she remembered she was the one who'd approached them.

"You can read this?" she asked, raising a manicured eyebrow.

Finn nodded. "It's in the language of my people. Well, mine and a couple other races. Why did you show it to me?"

She swallowed, then glanced down at the note. "Because I don't know what it says, and you have markings on the side of your head that match the note. I thought you might be able to read it."

Finn and Penny glanced at one another.

"You can see the marks on my head?" He lifted his hair and turned to give her a better look.

She stared, her face scrunching, then leaned in, the bat still between them. "What the hell? I swear you had runes tattooed on the side of your head earlier."

Finn's hopes fell slightly. He did have runes tattooed on the side of his head, but they were only visible if the person looking at them was a magic-user. This woman obviously wasn't, and neither was the clerk in the store. The guy who'd hit him with his truck had been odd, but Finn was pretty sure he wasn't a user, either.

Earth was turning out to be nothing like he thought it was going to be.

"You know, your friend is in real trouble, according to that note." Finn sighed and looked at Penny, who knew what he was about to say and gave a sigh of her own. "I'm guessing you don't have any experience finding people?"

"Not exactly, no."

"Tell you what, I'll make a deal with you. I'll help you find your friend if you help me navigate this odd place."

"This odd place?" She raised an eyebrow. "The Kum & Go?"

Finn furrowed his brow. "I thought you called this Earth?"

"Where are you from, exactly?"

"We hail from—"

Penny cut him off with a puff of flame and a stern look.

"Uh, Canada. We're from Canada."

"That actually explains a lot." She bit her lip and frowned at the note on her phone. "You say he's in trouble?"

"Afraid so. From the looks of it, he was kidnapped, but he knew it was coming. I have a ship with scanners that could find him, but I need a few parts to get it working." Finn smiled.

Penny smacked her forehead with a taloned hand.

"A ship? Like, a boat? In the mountains?" The bat was thrust into his face. "Who the fuck are you? No lying, just the straight truth." She pointed at Penny as an afterthought. "And what the hell is that?"

Finn and Penny exchanged looks. Finally, Finn shrugged, and Penny waved for him to continue. She crossed her arms and huffed.

"Well, as I said before your unplanned nap, this is Penny. She is one of the last Faerie Dragons in the universe and my stalwart companion." That elicited an eye roll from the little blue dragon, but Finn pressed on. "And I am Finnegan Dragonbender, third son of His Majesty, four hundred and sixty-seventh of Yimr, King of the Dwarves. You can just call me Finn." He held out his hand for her to shake.

The bat didn't waver as she stared at him, then down at Penny who was standing on his knee.

Penny nodded and flashed her a smile.

"One of three things is happening here." The woman

put the bat in her lap and held up a finger. "One, I've gone completely insane." She held up a second finger. "Two, *you're* completely insane, but have also trained a lizard that can breathe fire, and looks a whole lot like a dragon, to understand human speech." The third finger went up. "Or three, this is all true, and my friend is in real trouble, and you are the only person I've come across that knows how to find him."

She was quiet while she considered. Then she turned and started the car.

"Close the door and buckle up. And don't even think of trying anything, I have a taser, and I have no problem using it."

Finn smiled and pulled the door closed. After a second, he found the seatbelt and secured it with a click. "Where are we going?"

"My office," she said, pulling out of the gas station, and taking the entrance ramp to 70 East.

She punched the gas, and the Hellcat roared to life, rocketing them onto the freeway. Finn felt the thrill of power rumbling through his seat and let out a laugh of joy.

She smiled and glanced at him. "Mila. Mila Winters." She reached over and quickly shook his hand. She started to pull back but saw Penny had a small hand out ready to shake. To her credit, Mila only hesitated for a few seconds before offering a finger, which the dragon gripped and shook.

"It's a pleasure to meet you, Mila. This vehicle is quite invigorating." Finn was all smiles as they passed cars and underpasses.

"You are a strange man," she said, changing lanes with a quick flip of the turn signal.

"I'm not a man. I'm a dwarf."

Mila shook her head. "Dude, you can't say that. They're 'little people,'" she mumbled.

CHAPTER SIX

"Why don't you use the towers for housing like everyone else?" Finn asked, staring out the window at the passing city. "Having a city spread out this way seems like a poor use of resources."

"Towers?" Mila said, cocking her head to the side. "I mean, there are skyscrapers downtown, but those are mostly businesses. I suppose a lot of people live in them, too. Do people from Canada live in towers?"

"What?" Finn looked her way and caught Penny giving him the eye. "Oh, uh, yeah. I suppose they do."

"How long have you been in the states?" Mila asked, switching to the exit lane.

"The States? I don't follow. What are the states?" Finn felt he was starting to lose her, but he was so far out of the loop, he wasn't aware there was a loop to begin with. The only information he knew about Earth people and places was from the black and white movies he had recorded from TV signals he and Penny had happened to find. He was starting to think those movies were rather old, and perhaps a little out of date.

Mila gave him a sidelong glance. "The United States of America. The country we're currently in?"

Finn saw her look. He'd better play it cool, or she was going to reconsider helping him.

He gave a forced chuckle. "Oh. Up in Canada, we call it The United. We've been here for about three hours."

Mila laughed. "Three hours? What were you driving, a jet or something? I thought you had a boat."

"No."

Finn didn't know what else to say. This place was very confusing to him. There didn't seem to be any magic, even though everyone he had come across so far had shown that they themselves had the ability to use magic. He could see the aura around them all from the corner of his eye, but not one of them so far had shown the slightest magical ability. He decided a change of subject would be better.

"So, what is it you do, Mila Winters?"

"I'm an anthropologist at the Museum of Nature and Science," she said, sitting up a little straighter in her seat.

"What's that?" Finn asked.

Mila shrank back down. "I find and study ancient civilizations and their cultures. I also study artifacts."

That caught Finn's attention. "You find artifacts? That's what me and Penny do!"

Mila took the exit for Colorado Street and turned right on a red light after checking for traffic. "You find artifacts? You're an archaeologist?"

"No, I'm a treasure hunter."

Mila was quiet, but the frown on her face was not a good sign.

Finn felt he better elaborate before whatever he had said was taken wrong. "We do research on lost or stolen objects and find out where they were taken, then we take them back."

That seemed to mollify her. "So, you're not a grave robber?"

Finn had done his fair share of grave robbing, but only when the object was important enough that if it were lost forever, it would be a tragedy. Or if it didn't hurt anybody. And he only went after dwarven-made objects, which, according to dwarven law, all belonged to the royal family anyway. But he felt like here on Earth, "grave robber" was a dirty word.

"I'm sure some would label me that out of spite, but they're usually just mad that they didn't find the artifact first."

"What do you do with them? The artifacts?" Mila asked, turning into a large, open, green space with a huge, sleek building to the left. She turned left toward the building, taking the speed bumps slowly as the engine growled, wanting to be let loose.

"Usually, I give it back to whoever hired me to find it. But if it's too dangerous, I will return it to the family vault. Sometimes, if I'm working on my own, I sell them," Finn said, leaning down so he could see the whole building out the passenger-side window.

Mila pulled into a spot up front and shut the engine off. "That sounds suspiciously like you're a for-profit tomb raider."

Finn smiled and glanced her way. "Sort of. But I try to stay out of tombs on principle."

"I'm not going to lie, Finn. I don't know how I feel about that. But I need your help, so come on." She climbed out of the car and waited for Finn and Penny to follow before locking the doors.

She led him to a side entrance and used her key card to unlock it. Holding the door open for him, she motioned for him to enter. "After you. Take a right, then the second door on the left."

Finn walked past her, having to turn slightly sideways to fit past her and the door. Penny scurried up onto his shoulder and glanced over her wing before quietly saying, "Scrich, crii squeek?"

"I don't know that I *completely* trust her," he replied in a whisper, walking down the carpeted hall. "I just think she can help. Plus, what are the odds that one of the first people we meet is in need of someone who can read the dwarven script? It's fate."

Penny rolled her eyes so hard she nearly fell off his shoulder. "Chir? Squeech cri."

"I know you don't believe in fate," Finn held his hand up to forestall her, "but you have to admit that fate or luck or whatever you want to call it has played a huge part in us getting here. We picked up the radio and TV signals that no one else did, we had just enough in the *Anthem*'s tanks to get us here, then the first place we get dropped off, there is a woman looking for someone who reads dwarven because her friend is missing? Come on! Something is pushing us together. Besides, it's not like we have much choice. We need to find a Huldu and get the

Anthem back online, and this woman needs to find someone that our scanners would have no problem picking out. Fate."

Penny furrowed her eye ridges but nodded in agreement. "Sqee, sqee."

Finn smiled. "Okay, I'll keep my head about me, and you keep an eye out for anyone who's using magic. There has to be someone on Earth that still knows how to tap into the energies."

"This way," Mila called behind him.

Finn turned and realized he had walked right past the second door. He smiled and walked back. "Sorry, I was lost in conversation." He gestured at Penny, who bobbed her head in apology.

Mila's eyebrow raised slowly. "She can talk back?"

"Of course. Penny is one of the smartest people I know." He held up his fist, and Penny bumped it with her tiny one.

Mila just shook her head and walked through the door. "This is crazy."

Finn followed her in and stopped when the lights came on automatically. The room was two stories tall, and large enough that an elephant could walk around without hitting a wall. There was a long table in the center covered in artifacts that ranged from old, rusted weapons to pottery with vibrant paintings encircling them. At least twenty artifacts were in various stages of being cleaned and documented on a second table, and the walls held shelves upon shelves of objects of all descriptions.

Mila walked to a desk that was immaculately clean and organized. She opened a drawer and pulled out an envelope and a pad of paper, then plucked a pen from a mug full of writing utensils. She brought them to a clear spot at the center table and set them down.

"Okay, that's the original letter. If you can translate it for me, I'll answer any questions you have." She pulled a tall stool over for Finn, then went to the corner and started filling a coffee urn with water. "You want some coffee? I need to wake up. I have a feeling I'm not going to sleep much tonight."

Finn had no idea what coffee was, but he agreed to a cup and sat at the table to get started on the translation for her.

By the time the room was filled with an earthy aroma that made Finn's mouth water, he had the translated note written out for Mila.

"That smells amazing. What is it?" Finn asked, taking the cup she offered him.

Mila's brow furrowed. "It's coffee. Don't tell me you've never had coffee. What are you, Mormon or something?"

Finn took a gulp to avoid having to answer.

"Whoa! Calm down there, you're going to burn yourself!" Mila shrieked, making Finn jerk and take a bigger gulp than he had intended.

The liquid was hot, but being a dwarf, he was able to handle more intense temperatures than Peabrains. He swallowed the mouthful and marveled at the bitter taste. It was one of the best things he had ever drunk. He quickly gulped the rest down as Mila stared at him in shocked horror.

Finn smacked his lips and held out the mug. "That is delightful! Is there any more?"

Mila, whose mouth was still open in shock, took the

mug. "How the fuck did you do that? That was nearly boiling when I poured it."

"I'm a dwarf. I told you that." Finn shrugged. "We have much hardier bodies than your kind."

Mila turned woodenly and returned to the counter to refill his mug.

"This is insane," she said, staring at the steaming mug. "I'll admit, the dragon was pretty convincing, but I could explain that away by thinking she was just some rare species of lizard I've never heard of before." She turned back to hand him the second cup of coffee. "But I have never seen or heard of anyone who can drink near-boiling liquid like it's room temperature. That's what did it. Just so you know. The coffee. I believe you. You're a dwarf. Like a 'and my axe!' sort of dwarf. Congratulations. You broke me." She held up her mug so he could clink it.

Finn frowned but clinked mugs with her. "I'm sorry I broke you. What do you mean?"

"I believe you. I don't know if it's the long day and lack of sleep, but for whatever reason, I believe you are a dwarf king. Or prince, or whatever."

Finn was amazed to see the calm that had come over the small woman. It was as if she had changed her whole outlook on the world in one go. Even Penny was a little wide-eyed at the change.

"Um, okay." Finn took a gulp of coffee and set the mug down on the table. "Is there anything I can do to make this a little easier for you?"

Penny slipped off his shoulder and stuck her head in the mug to get a taste. She pulled her head back after a gulp of her own and made a sour face. "Sre-blech."

Mila raised an eyebrow at the reaction, and Finn translated. "She doesn't like it. It's too bitter. She prefers sweet or salty, but stays away from the bitter stuff."

Mila thought for a second, then went to a small fridge under the counter and squatted as she opened it. She returned with a thin, tall yellow box and opened the top. She shook out several miniature chocolate bars about three-quarters of an inch long and a quarter-inch thick.

"Give these a try. I had a student assistant this summer who loved them." Mila offered the box to Finn.

He took it and read the label. Charleston Chew Minis. He shook a few into his hand and popped them into his mouth. They were cold from being in the freezer, so when he bit down, they shattered into a million pieces and quickly melted in his mouth.

Finn's eyes widened as the sweet nougat and chocolaty goodness overtook his taste buds. "These are amazing!"

Penny was making similar sounds, dancing in a circle, and throwing another mini in her mouth.

"Well, you guys can have them. I don't really like candy," Mila said, pulling up another stool and sitting beside Finn. "Now, what does this note say?"

She picked up the translation and started reading as Finn had the brilliant idea to drop a few of the chews into his coffee, then take a sip.

"Oh, now that's amazing." He mumbled before taking a large gulp.

CHAPTER SEVEN

Mila,

If you are reading this, I have been taken. I hate to have to put this on you, but if you are able to find someone to translate this note, you are one step closer than anyone else would be able to get. I have seen the magic in you, although you don't know it's there. I have full faith that you will work tirelessly until you can understand these words.

To the being who is reading this note, there is darkness coming. The Black Star is what they call themselves, and they plan on carving up this world and creating a magical nation. They will build it on a foundation of dead bodies if they must. They have, I believe, mastered dark magic and are able to practice it without being consumed.

I need not emphasize what this would mean for all of us Magicals, let alone the Peabrains.

I believe I have been taken due to my ability to find and activate dwarven-made artifacts, a skill I now regret cultivating. The Black Star's minions have approached me over the last few months and made me offers, but I could not join them in good conscience. I did take their money in exchange for some work, though, which I now fear might have been my death sentence.

I am certain that the Black Star is somewhere in northern Europe or western Russia. They have located far too many artifacts on their own for them to be looking anywhere else.

If you are reading this, please forgive my weakness. I needed the money. But with me gone, they will be moving up their plans. Alert the Huldu. They will know what to do.

I'm sorry.

Jeffery.

M ila put the note down and quietly sipped her coffee while she processed.

Finn wondered what she would ask about first. He was betting on the part where Jeff talked about "us Magicals."

She bit her lip and turned to him. "What's a Peabrain?"

That made Finn's eyebrows go up. "That's what you are. You're a Peabrain."

Her brow furrowed. "I have a feeling that word means something different to you than it does to me."

"It's a reference to your magical brain." He held his thumb and forefinger so there was a small gap. "It's very small but potent. You all have one, but for some reason, you can't seem to access it."

"My magical brain?" Mila raised an eyebrow.

"Yeah." Finn ate another of the chews, and Penny did the same, smiling with chocolate on her teeth.

"*Magic.* You're telling me magic is real?"

Finn nodded, and Mila nodded along with him.

"Okay, big fella. Show me some magic." She crossed her leg over her knee and turned to face him, wearing a look of expectancy behind her mug of coffee.

"Oh. Uh, I suppose I can show you something."

Finn patted his jacket, looking for something to do a simple spell with. Then he remembered he was wearing his adventuring harness, and reached to the small of his back and pulled out the handle of his axe.

"Okay, this is dwarven weapon magic. Mila, meet Fragar."

Finn held the leather-wrapped handle close to Mila's face so she wouldn't miss anything and gave her a smile. Her expression didn't change; it was still judging him for not having done any magic so far.

Finn whispered the power word under his breath. In less than a second, the handle grew, and Fragar flipped open, glowing purple and covered in runes.

Mila squeaked and fell backward off her stool. Finn leapt to his feet and grabbed the front of her jacket to keep her from hitting the ground. Mila's coffee spilled down the front of her, soaking her t-shirt and jacket, but she hung a few inches from the carpet, undamaged, her eyes wide.

"Are you okay?" Finn asked, still holding Fragar in his free hand.

Mila dropped her mug, her arms flailing as she tried to right herself, but unable to find any purchase. She gave him a dirty look. "You could have warned me, motherfucker! Now I have a wet shirt, and I might have peed myself. Pull me up."

Finn's face reddened with embarrassment, and he

hauled her up by the jacket until she was seated once again. She tried to wipe the coffee off her front, but it had thoroughly soaked through her gray shirt, making a dark line down the middle where her jacket hadn't protected it.

"Sorry. I forget how abrupt the transformation can look. To me, it's just a tool I can summon. So, that was the first bit of magic you've ever seen?"

Finn sat back down and reached for his coffee, but found Penny piling mini chews into it and stirring it with the pen he had used to translate the note.

"What the hell?"

"Chi, chi!" she said, then stuck her snout in and took a drink.

"Yeah, I know adding the candies made it better, but now you're just ruining it."

Penny frowned, shrugged, and took another long sip.

Mila hopped off her stool and picked up the empty mug. She took it to the small sink at the counter, then walked to a cabinet beside her desk. She opened it, and Finn saw that it was full of clothes on hangers. She selected a white V-neck tee and a short, red leather jacket. She turned and walked out the door.

"Uh, where are you going?" Finn asked, not sure if he should follow or not.

"Just stay there," she called from the hall. "I'm just getting out of these wet clothes."

Finn reached for his coffee again, but Penny blocked him with her body, her eyes a little wild.

"Okay. I'll just get my own, I guess."

Penny smiled and stuck her head in the mug to get to the now significantly drained contents.

Finn walked to the counter and found a clean mug in a cupboard that said Anthropologists like it civilized. He set Fragar on the counter and filled the mug with the black brew from the steaming pot.

"Motherfucker!" Mila shouted from the hall.

"What's the matter?" Finn asked, snatching up Fragar and dropping into a fighting stance.

"My bra is soaked in coffee, and I don't have a spare one here. Dammit! This is my favorite one. Fuck it, I needed to get more anyway. Should probably get an extra one for the office while I'm out."

Finn relaxed and returned to his stool, raising an eyebrow at Penny, who was smiling maniacally beside the now-empty mug and nearly vibrating with energy.

"What's wrong with you?"

"Cheeee! Shir chip shee!" She blew a white-hot flame and several smoke rings from each nostril to punctuate her decree.

Finn frowned and looked down at the steaming black liquid. "I guess I feel more awake, but I wouldn't say I feel invincible. Maybe this stuff has some sort of side effect?"

Mila came back in, her brows rising at the sight of Penny dancing in a circle around her mug as if she were a druid trying to summon the Tree Father.

"You look nice." Finn smiled and nodded.

Mila was now wearing the red jacket zipped up past her chest, hiding all but the bottom of her white shirt that hugged her hips past the short jacket's hem.

She blushed slightly. "Thanks. It's better than a white shirt and no bra." She went to the sink and began rinsing out her coffee-stained clothing. Finn watched, not sure what the woman was thinking, but glad she hadn't thrown him out yet.

He smiled. "Fate," he said quietly into his coffee before taking another drink of the bitter brew.

"What's wrong with Penny?" Mila asked over her shoulder, her eyes a little wide.

The dragon had moved from dancing to flying in loops around the room. She was picking up speed, and beginning to hum some kind of epic tune that sounded suspiciously like *Flight of the Valkyries*.

"I think the coffee is having a strange effect on her." Finn followed her progress, becoming concerned by his friend's manic behavior.

"How much did she drink?" Mila wrung out the shirt and jacket and hung them on the cabinets' door handles. After a second, she shrugged and hung the nude-colored bra on one as well.

"The whole cup." Finn picked it up and saw that she had also scraped out the melted chews in the bottom. "She also had ten or fifteen of the chews."

"What?" Mila spun, her eyes wide as she tracked Penny's progress around the room. "She drank the whole thing? No wonder she's probably buzzed out of her mind. You can't have that much caffeine and not expect to jump off the walls."

Finn looked into his own mug, suddenly suspicious of the delicious drink. "What's caffeine?"

Mila covered her eyes with one hand and sighed. "You know what? This night just keeps getting weirder and weirder. I need a drink. How about you?"

Finn perked up at that. "I could most certainly use a good whiskey. Do you have that here?"

She furrowed her brow. "Yeah, man. We have whiskey here." She motioned for him to follow. "Come on. And please put that axe away."

Finn smiled and whispered the power word. In an instant, the axe folded back up into a small, leather-covered piece of wood. He slipped Fragar into its holster at the small of his back and downed the coffee in one go.

"Wait, before we go, do you have a picture of Jeff?"

She thought about that for a second, then nodded. "Yeah, a picture from our last dig together. It's hanging in his office." She motioned for him to follow her and stepped into the hall.

Finn looked up to see Penny doing a flip. "Come on. We need to get you a drink."

"Chip shee," Penny protested, landing on his shoulder and pouting.

"I know liquor puts you to sleep. That's the idea." He walked out into the hall and saw Mila waiting at a door a few feet down and on the opposite side of the hall.

"In here."

He followed her into a workspace nearly identical to her own, except that there were no artifacts, and the desk was a mess of paperwork and food wrappers.

Mila pointed to a picture on the wall. "This was taken last year, at a site in Mexico. A lot of good finds on that trip."

Finn leaned in to get a better look, and both he and Penny sucked in a breath.

"What is it?" Mila asked, her smile fading to a worried look.

Finn leaned in more just to be sure. There were several nonmagical races in the universe, and for the most part, they kept to themselves. However, some interaction was inevitable, and Magicals found out very quickly that the nonmagical races didn't exactly welcome them with open arms. Over time, Magicals found spells that could hide their nature from those that couldn't see past the illusions. The spells were simple and easy for any magic users, even children, but they didn't work on other Magicals. The concealment spell worked even in photos and video but created a strange double image for any Magical who viewed it, revealing both their true and concealed forms.

In the photo were Mila and a huge man in the middle of a jungle, with several pits dug up and marked off with twine grids behind them. The man was not fat, but not exactly fit either. It was hard to tell how tall he was, due to them both squatting next to an excavation site, but even in that position, he was a good two heads taller than Mila. His toothy grin made him look somewhat simple, if not jovial.

Finn and Penny saw something else in addition to the happy man at Mila's side. There was a sort of image over-laying the physical image of what Jeffery really was. It was close to the truth but translated into human features.

"He's a troll," Finn said, taking the photo frame from the wall and shaking his head.

"He's not that bad. I know he has some trouble with the ladies, but he's actually really nice," Mila defended her coworker, putting her hand on her hip and daring Finn to say different.

"No, I mean, he's an actual troll. He's using a conceal-ment spell, but I can see his true form under the image." Finn frowned and held up the photo for her to look at, while Penny nodded in agreement a little faster than she normally would.

Mila leaned in and looked closer, but after a second, she shook her head. "What are you talking about?"

Finn turned the picture so they could both see it and pointed at Jeff's face. "You don't see his tusks?"

"Tusks?" Mila threw her hands up. "Now you're just making shit up."

Finn was a little disappointed but not really surprised. "I just figured if you were able to see my tattoos, you have to have a little magic active, but maybe not."

He opened the back of the frame and took the picture out. On the back in blue pen was written, *Jeff and Mila, Mexico, Mayan dig site 34.*

"Can I hang onto this? Might need it to show some people, if I can ever find a market on this planet."

"On this *planet?*" Mila blinked slowly. "Okay. Time for that drink. Let's go. No talking in the car. I need to process the last hour of my life."

CHAPTER EIGHT

Finn rode quietly in the passenger seat as they drove for about ten minutes, winding through a city that frankly didn't make a whole lot of sense to him. How could the entire Peabrain population of Earth forget they had magic? He was sure they had *forgotten*, not lost the power. He could see the magical auras from the corner of his eyes, surrounding everyone they passed.

He checked Mila several times, glancing her way without ever actually looking at her, and sure enough, she had a glow. It didn't make sense. She had seen his tattoos, so he knew she could at least access the power, even if not consciously.

Finn rested his chin on his thumb, his elbow on the door's armrest, and watched a city completely built and maintained with technology. Not a single bit of magic was on display, and frankly, he was finding it a bit disturbing.

Penny sat on his knee, vibrating with caffeinated energy, staring out the windshield, snapping her head toward any movement she saw. Finn would be worried, but he had seen her much worse off. Like the one time they had accidentally made soup with the mushrooms he had stolen from the evil priests of Grothan. Turned out the visions were not from divine visitation, but of a more fungal nature. Luckily, his dwarven constitution required a whole lot to be overridden; he had eaten four bowls of the stuff, and only felt a slight buzz...to his mild disappointment.

Finn glanced at Mila, who had both hands on the wheel, and was staring straight ahead. She didn't seem upset, per se, but she wasn't exactly smiling either. He hoped she wouldn't just leave them to their own devices. He was sure that fate was wielding her influence like a bull in a china shop.

That thought gave him comfort that everything would work out. Things usually did, he found, when he let them play out.

Finn took the opportunity to really look at the woman who had decided to help instead of leaving him in the parking lot of a Kum & Go.

She was pretty. Probably the prettiest woman he had ever seen in real life. She was short but had an air about her he liked that made her seem larger than life. Her long black hair and olive skin complemented each other well, especially against the red leather of her jacket. She was obviously adventurous if the smile on her face in the photo of her and Jeff was any indication, and she wasn't someone who ran from adversity. Her pulling out a bat and shoving it in his face was a pretty good sign of that.

She was smart, too. He had seen a certificate on her office wall saying she held a Ph.D. in anthropology, something he assumed was a high honor if the paper was displayed for all to see. He liked smart. It was the reason he and Penny got along so well. Penny and Mila were probably equal when it came to brains, though he bet that neither one of them would admit it to the other.

There was a problem Finn had come across in his years of travel when it came to smart people. They tended to not believe the unbelievable. They didn't like to be wrong, so they rejected anything that didn't fit into their worldview. It was a flaw in Finn's eyes.

Believing the unbelievable was how he had gotten so far in life, it was how he had gone and found Penny, and why he never stopped looking for *Earth*. Finn knew he was smart as well, but his smarts were of a much more specific nature.

He was a dwarf. He was taught to be fair and just at all costs. Sometimes, the only way to be fair and just was to kill a bunch of people, so every dwarf was taught the art of war from a very young age. In battle, Finn was a genius.

But this woman beside him broke the norm over her knee—at least, so far, she had. He couldn't imagine what was going through her mind. He had told her magic was real, then showed her some, and instead of running for the hills like the store clerk had earlier, she seemed to be absorbing it, or at least trying to reason it out.

"Can I ask you something?" Mila said, not taking her eyes off the road.

"Anything." Finn smiled, smoothing a stray beard hair down.

She licked her lips, then set her jaw. "Are you from another planet?"

Penny's head jerked over her wing as she stared daggers at him. He ignored her.

"Technically, everyone on *Earth* is from another planet. I mean, if you want to get really technical, this isn't even a planet."

They rode in silence as she took a turn on a red light and pulled up to the mouth of an alley.

"Get out."

Finn opened his mouth to protest, but she had every right to kick him out. He really needed to remember that these people had no idea that they were not alone in the universe.

His jaw clicked shut, and he opened the door. He was about to say something else, but stopped himself and climbed out.

The Hellcat growled and Mila turned down the alley, disappearing between the buildings. Finn wanted to run after her but stood his ground.

Penny sat on the ground, pointedly not looking at him, her jaw flexed as she clenched her teeth.

"What? I'm not going to lie to her." Finn crossed his arms, his stubborn nature rearing up. "She deserves to know the truth."

"Swii? Chir chee!" Penny flapped her wings and was suddenly hovering in his face, her pointer talon nearly poking him in the nose. "Chi squee! Griit shry?"

"Okay, 'deserves' might not be the right word, but she's smart. She would have seen through us eventually. I didn't want to lie to her." He waved his hand in front of his face to bat away her talon. "She's not an asset we needed, neces-sarily. This is the goal." He spread his hands, encompassing everything they could see. "*Earth*! We found it. This was the whole goal. Now you're pissed that I told a Peabrain what she should already know?"

Penny frowned but didn't argue. She instead landed on his shoulder and sagged in defeat. Finn turned and started slowly walking down the street.

"The bar is this way, big guy."

Mila's voice broke through his sudden depression like a light in a dark room.

He spun and saw she was standing on the corner to the alley, pointing in the opposite direction.

"I thought you were done with us?" Finn asked, confused.

"No, I needed to park the car, and there wouldn't have been enough room for you to get out because I needed to park close to the wall so my roommate can fit her car in as well." She raised an eyebrow. "You thought I would just kick you two out in the middle of a strange city? Who do you think I am?"

Finn walked up and fell in beside her as she started down the sidewalk. "I just figured the talk of not being from here and all was just a bit too much."

"I'm not going to lie. That seems a bit far-fetched, but I told you back at the Kum & Go that I was taking option three. I don't know why, but I believe you."

They rounded the corner and headed down 21st Street.

"Besides, the whole magical axe—"

"Fragar."

"Fragar was a pretty good show. I kinda want to see a little more before the ride is over. It's a little like fate wants us to work together."

Finn smiled and glanced at Penny, whose shoulders once again dropped in defeat.

"How so?" Finn prompted.

"I study ancient artifacts for a living. In all the years I've cataloged things or written theories on culture or dug objects up, I've seen things that didn't make a whole lot of sense." She turned them left down Market Street. "Sometimes we might find thirty artifacts in one spot, and twenty-nine of them are nothing but rusted-out shells, but the thirtieth is in nearly mint condition. Or we find buildings that are thousands of years too old to exist in the current theories of human development. Just strange things that I had to write off as some sort of anomaly. Until I met you two. If what you're saying is true, then that actually fits with my worldview, in a way."

They walked in silence, turning right on 20th, then left on Blake. Finn was about to say more when Mila pointed to a nondescript, one-story, brick building with the word "Refinery" in raised lettering on the side.

"Here we are." She pulled the door open and held it for them. "Uh, Penny, you might want to keep a low profile. It's a Wednesday and late, so it's probably pretty empty, but pets aren't allowed inside. Not saying you're a pet, but they'll see it that way."

Penny huffed two smoke rings, but crawled down into Finn's jacket and around his torso, hiding. Finn had a mesh, hammock-like bag attached to his adventuring harness for just this reason. He felt her settle into the bag just above Fragar.

"That was easier than I thought it was going to be." Mila was a little stunned.

"It's pretty normal for people to react badly at the sight of a Faerie Dragon. We have a system."

"Chii." Penny's voice was muffled, but the sass was clear.

"After you." Finn held the door, and let Mila take the lead.

The dark bar was fairly narrow and long, with a bar down the right side, and tables and chairs on the left. Several TVs were on the walls, but all of them had the volume down, and rock music played at a moderate level, giving the place an easygoing feeling without being too loud to have a conversation. The place was half neighborhood bar and half speakeasy.

About ten people were in the whole place, including the bored-looking bartender. He leaned against the counter, reading a paperback, and drinking a beer. He wore a short-billed cap, his curly, brown hair sticking out the side. A black vest covered a white button-up shirt, giving him a dapper look.

Mila walked up to the bar, and the guy brightened up.

"Oi, good ta see ye, lass."

The bartender's accent reminded Finn of home, but was slightly harsher. He put the book and beer down and came over to greet Mila.

"Hey, Danny. How's it going tonight?" Mila was all smiles as she shook his hand.

"Good, fer a Wednesday. Danica's over in de carner if yer lookin' for 'er," he said, wiping his hands on a bar towel and flipping it onto his shoulder.

"Shit. I thought she had to work tomorrow."

Mila looked over her shoulder at a tall blonde woman

sitting at a corner high-top table, talking with three good-looking men. They seemed to be completely fascinated by her.

"Danica?" Finn asked, following her gaze.

He saw a table in the corner where a blonde elf woman and three Peabrains were chatting each other up.

Finn raised an eyebrow.

"My roommate. She's the gorgeous blonde in the corner. I thought she was at home. It's fine, we can just take a booth. I'll talk to her later."

"Who's this big gob whicha, den?" Danny asked, eyeing Finn.

"Oh, this is my…friend, Finn. He's new in town." Mila only hesitated a second before saying "friend."

"Finn? Dat's a good Scottish name if I air herd one. Ye from the homeland by chance?" he asked, reaching over the bar and shaking Finn's hand.

"Afraid not." Finn smiled. "Canada."

"Too bad. Thought I might'nt be alone 'ere fer a minute." He smacked his hands together and rubbed them together vigorously. "What can ol' Danny get ye?"

"G &T for me," Mila said, looking to Finn.

"Whiskey. Actually, I'll take two of them."

"Ye want a double?" Danny clarified, starting on the gin and tonic.

"No, two glasses, if you don't mind." Finn chuckled, hoping that would be enough.

"Aye. I kin do that," he said without batting an eye. He slid Mila's drink to her and poured two whiskeys, handing them to Finn.

A talon in his back made Finn jump slightly. "Do you have any snacks?"

Danny pointed to a bowl of peanuts. Finn nodded his thanks and, holding the two whiskeys in one hand, grabbed the bowl. He gave Danny a half salute with the bowl, and Danny nodded, picking his paperback up and leaning against the counter again.

Mila led them to a booth against the far wall and slid in. Finn followed on the opposite side, putting the peanuts against the wall, along with one of the whiskeys.

"Okay, you can come out, but keep it flame-free." Finn held his leather jacket open.

Penny shot out and practically dove into the bowl, covering herself in nuts and loudly crunching.

"Don't forget your whiskey. You need to bring it down about twelve notches."

"I guess I don't want any nuts anyway." Mila made a disgusted face, watching Penny practically swimming in the snack bowl.

Penny stopped rolling, and her head popped out. She stared at Mila for a second before saying, "Spi" in a quiet voice. Then the head sank back in, and she went back to eating.

"She said 'sorry,'" Finn translated.

"It's fine." Mila took a sip. "Okay, let me have it. I want the whole story. In for a penny, in for a pound."

"What does Penny have to do with pounds?" Finn raised an eyebrow, confused.

"No, it's an expression. It means I'm all in, so lay it on me. From the beginning."

Finn took a sip of whiskey and did as she asked.

CHAPTER NINE

Finn told her everything. He started with being the third son of the king, and how he went out to find his own fortunes when the family could find no use for him beyond window dressing for the court. He told of a few adventures where he had nearly died due to his rash actions. He moved on from there and relayed how he had rescued Penny from a cult that was intent on sacrificing her to their dark god, and how that had led them to a deal of mutual benefit. He had agreed to help Penny find a hoard so that she could finally lay her eggs and hopefully begin the long process of restoring her race's dwindling numbers.

That was when he realized how good she was at strategy and research. Their finds doubled quickly, and they made a bit of a name for themselves in the treasure-hunting communities.

The whole while, he had been obsessed with finding the lost luxury ship, *Earth*. Years later, he had been using the scanner, accidentally on the low-band setting, and that was when he began picking up radio and TV signals from *Earth*. From that point on, it became their mission to find the lost ship, and bring back some of the fabled riches as proof.

He finally told her about the signal from the engines that had led them here, explaining that when they warped in, they were too low, and got caught in *Earth*'s gravity well, and crash-landed.

"That nice man in the truck dropped us off at the refueling station, and you know the rest," Finn finished, taking a sip to wet his dry throat.

Mila hadn't said a word through the whole monologue, just sipped her drink and listened. Finn could tell that she had stopped herself several times from interrupting, but now that he was done, she wasn't saying anything.

"Are you okay? I know that was a lot of info all at once," Finn prompted.

"Cheer?" Penny said from the now-empty bowl she was using as a chaise lounge, her tail flipping contentedly over the rim.

"No." Finn rolled his eyes. "I don't think I broke her."

"I'm not going to lie," Mila finally said. "You came pretty close. How am I supposed to believe that there is a whole universe out there full of dwarves and elves and shit, and I just can't see them?" She shook her head, and Finn took the question to be rhetorical.

Several people had come in the bar since Finn had started his story. He hadn't stopped to look them all over, but now two men approached cautiously, standing a respectable distance away, waiting to talk.

Finn glanced their way and saw that they were elves.

He waved them over and gave them a big smile through his beard. "Hello, gentlemen."

The elves approached with looks of shock on their faces. The first opened his mouth to talk, but his friend elbowed him and indicated Mila. "Not in front of the Peabrain," he whispered.

"It's fine," Finn reassured them. "She's in the know, as it were." He jerked a thumb at Penny, who gave the two newcomers a wave and a smile.

"Very well," the first elf said with a slight bow. "We happened to see you when we entered, and to be honest, we couldn't believe our eyes. Not only a dwarf, but a royal? How is this possible?"

Finn cocked his head to the side slightly. "Why is seeing a dwarf such an odd thing? There were several on the original journey."

"True, but that was ages ago." The second elf, a wood elf if his brown ponytail was any indication, frowned apologetically. "The younger races haven't ever seen a dwarf. The last, who went by the name Leif Erikson, died nearly a thousand years ago."

"I'm sorry," Mila cut in, raising her hand for them to stop, "but you're saying that the first European in the Americas was a dwarf? And that he was the last?"

"Yes, ma'am." His brown ponytail bobbed with a nod.

Mila frowned. "But Leif Erikson had two kids, one of whom became chieftain of their tribe."

The first elf, a blond high elf, nodded. "That was true, but they were both Peabrains. He never had the chance to have a dwarven son with his wife."

Mila closed her eyes, shaking her head and trying to

make what he had said work. "If he had a son with a Peabr...human, wouldn't that child be half-human, half-dwarf?"

Finn looked past the two elves when movement at the bar caught his eye. Three people had come in some time ago, two men and a woman, and they had taken up residence at the bar. The woman was seated between the two young men, who were obviously making advances toward her. He hadn't taken much notice at first because she seemed fine with the attention, but as the night had gone on, she had become more uncomfortable. It looked as though the two men were trying to pressure her into something she wasn't down for.

The blond elf continued explaining the details of mixed races without noticing Finn's distracted manner.

Finn watched the woman and two men, reading body language and not liking what he was seeing. Finally, the woman spun on her stool and hopped off. He saw one of the guys starting to reach for her arm, which made Finn tense for action, but the other guy shook his head and they let her go. He leaned out of the booth slightly and saw that she was heading for the bathrooms.

The two men quietly argued for a second, then one of them pulled a small tube out of his pocket and glanced around, not noticing Finn from across the room. He popped the top off the tube and pulled a pill out, which he quickly and discreetly dropped into the woman's drink. He quickly stuffed the tube back into his pocket, and the two men smiled knowingly before clinking beer bottles and taking drinks.

"Excuse me," Finn interrupted the elves' lecture on the

mating habits of, well...everything. "Mila. Is there some custom here where men will drop a tablet into a woman's drink?"

Mila's eyes went wide. "Yeah, it's called date rape. Did you see that happen just now?" she half-stood, but the table was in the way, and the two elves, who both had disgusted looks on their faces as they scanned the room, were blocking her view.

"I did." Finn pushed out of the booth, Penny scrambling to get onto his shoulder before he was up. Gently guiding the elves to the side, he held out a hand for Mila and helped her out of the booth. "The woman is in the bathroom right now. If you would go in and tell her what is happening, I will take care of the assholes. She has red hair and is wearing a short black dress."

Mila gritted her teeth, looking past Finn at the two men at the bar. "Fucking pieces of shit," she spat at them before making a beeline for the bathroom.

"Can you two help me?" he asked the wood elf and the high elf standing next to him. "I assume there is an easy way to get hold of the authorities?"

"Yeah, I can call." The blond one nodded and pulled out a phone. "What should I tell them?"

Finn smiled. "Tell them that two guys just attacked a third while the three were having a conversation at a bar."

"Lying to the cops isn't a good idea." He hesitated, his thumb over the call button, then 911 dialed.

"Oh, that won't be a problem." Finn cracked the knuckles on each hand. "They're going to be the aggressors. Don't worry about that." He started forward, but stopped and turned back to the wood elf, who waited while his friend held the phone to his ear. "Before this gets out of hand, would you happen to know where I can find a Huldu?"

The wood elf blinked a couple of times, processing the question that had come out of the blue. "Uh, there's a market for Magicals just across the street. You'll need to go down the alley between Blake and Wazee streets. You can't miss it; it's about halfway down on the brick wall behind the bodega."

"Thanks, that helps a lot." Finn gave him a nod.

"Oh, there's a password," the elf added. "It's 'Peabrains are forgetful.'"

Finn smiled. "Thanks again."

He saw that the two guys at the bar were now looking his way after all the commotion. Or they might have just been staring at Penny, who now perched on his shoulder in plain view. Finn didn't really care. The fact that they'd noticed him was an advantage.

He walked up to the two and looked them over. He knew their type. They were the same on every world. Their buttons were going to be easy to push.

"Can we help you, fella?" the bald one on the left said, his thin mustache and short-cropped beard an offense to bearded men everywhere.

His friend, the one who had done the dosing, sneered and ran his hand through his short curly black hair.

"I doubt it," Finn said in a calm but condescending tone. "I'm betting that the two of you put together are dumber than the stools you're sitting on. More worthless, too. At least the stool is good for something, even if it's to keep your ugly asses from hitting the floor."

"Excuse me?" Curly said, his eyes narrowing.

"Did you fart?" Finn asked, raising an eyebrow and staring the man down.

Baldy stood up, nearly bumping chests with Finn. He was taller than Finn had originally thought, standing almost an inch taller than him. But where this guy was tall, he was also a little lanky.

"I don't think I like your tone, asshole." Baldy leaned into Finn's face, trying to intimidate him, but Finn just smiled.

"Well, I don't like that you're wasting valuable resources *existing*, but the real question is, what are you going to do about it, little fella?"

A talon poked into his shoulder from the very still dragon was all the warning he needed. He and Penny had long ago set up a system when confronting two people. He got in one's face, and Penny watched the other one. More times than not, the sucker punch came from the second guy, like this time.

Finn had to give Curly props for how fast he could move, but Finn was faster. While his friend had been in Finn's face, Curly stood and swung a punch at him, using Baldy to block most of his movements.

Instead of stepping back to avoid the punch, Finn just flexed his jaw tight and bowed his head. Turning slightly, he lined up so that Curly's fist would hit him on the crown of his head instead of the face.

Dwarves have very thick skulls and extremely strong neck muscles, so there was no give for Curly's fist. A loud cracking sound told Finn that his hand was broken in at least one place.

A blood-curdling scream from Curly cut through the music and made everyone in the bar turn to see Finn standing face to face with the bald man and his friend holding a hand with two of the digits pointing the wrong way.

Baldy blinked, not entirely sure what had just happened but willing to play. He stepped back and threw a punch at Finn.

Finn snapped his own fist out and hit Baldy's incoming fist square on. The move was so weird that Baldy didn't see it coming, and again the denser dwarf won the contest. Baldy's wrist snapped as if he had just punched a moving car, and Baldy joined his friend in screaming.

Finn reached past them and held the woman's drink between the two men. "I just want you to be sure you know why this is happening to you."

The wide-eyed looks on their faces told the whole story.

"Oi, what the feck is go'n on 'ere?" Danny shouted, coming down the bar, his paperback replaced by a bat.

Finn set the drink back down and slid it to Danny. "These two assholes just drugged a woman's drink when she went to the restroom."

"They've been pushing me to sleep with both of them all night," the redheaded woman said, stomping toward Finn and the other two. Mila jogged to catch up, and Danica was behind her. "I can't believe you would do that, Tony!" She stepped past Finn and punched the curly-haired guy in the nose.

Finn was impressed. It was a solid punch and made

Tony stumble back to fall over a stool, clutching his face with his unbroken hand.

Baldy knew the jig was up. He took off for the door, but Finn tripped him as he passed, and he tumbled to the floor. Not used to a broken wrist, he threw both arms out to stop himself, and screamed again when his awkwardly bent wrist bent even farther and something snapped further up in his arm. He rolled over, clutching the now-broken arm, tears of pain welling in his eyes.

Mila stepped up next to Finn with a smile on her face. "Damn, Finn. When you said you'd take care of it, I thought you meant you were going to have them kicked out, not kick their asses."

"I didn't kick anyone's ass. They did this to themselves. Mostly." Finn shrugged his indifference.

Danny came around the bar to stand over the two beaten and bloody men. He frowned, looking at the two, then at the redheaded woman. "Lass, I'm sorry this happened in my establishment. Believe me, I'll be sure the coppers handle this proper." He turned to Finn and Mila. "You two better get out of 'ere before I call 'em. No need havin' ya two bogged down in all this. Plus, at this time eh night, they like to just take in everyone involved and sart it out in te marnin. Come 'round again, an' I'll be buyin' the drinks."

"Oh, I already had my friends over there call the authorities. They should be here any minute." Finn pointed to the two elves, who gave Danny a wave.

"Right, then we should go now," Mila said, pulling Finn's arm and heading for the door. "The last thing I need at work is to answer why I ended up spending the night in jail."

"Hey, I'm coming with you!" A melodic voice rang out behind them, followed by the tapping of heels.

Finn looked back and saw Danica quickly walking their way, waving for them to slow down.

"Oh, shit." Mila hung her head but kept walking until they were out the door and on the sidewalk.

"Do you not like your roommate?" Finn asked, confused as to why she seemed so reluctant to let Danica join them.

"No, I love her!" she quickly corrected. "I just don't know how I will explain who you are to her. She's pretty sheltered when it comes to anything but flirting or medical stuff."

The night was cool and quiet, but a city as big as Denver was never really silent, as the approaching sirens attested.

"Come on, let's get out of here." She tried to pull him down the street, back toward where she had parked her car, but Finn stopped her.

"Actually, I want to make a stop if you don't mind. It shouldn't take long." She held onto his arm but followed instead of led as he crossed the empty street.

The door to the bar swung open, and the clicking of heels on concrete told them that Danica had made it outside. "Guys! Wait up."

Finn stopped and waited for the tall elven woman. She was beautiful and lithe, like most elves, and her blonde hair and long ears told Finn that she was either a high elf, or a moon elf. She wore a frilly, white top that exposed her collarbone and shoulders and was held up by some sort of elastic band. The shirt exposed her midriff, which complemented her low-rise blue jeans. She topped the whole thing off with a pair of white stilettos. They had to be some of the most impractical shoes Finn had ever seen, but he had to admit they did wonders for her long legs.

Mila sighed and waited, not seeming to notice that she hadn't let go of Finn's arm.

"Hey, guys." Danica's smile faltered when she got a good look at Finn. She stared, then leaned to the side to read the runes tattooed below the short hair on the sides of his head. Presumably they would be visible to her.

Finn turned his head slightly so she would have an uninterrupted view. "Hello. I'm Finnegan Dragonbender, or Finn to my friends. And this is Penny." Penny gave a small burst of flame in greeting.

Danica jumped a little at the flame, but it wasn't nearly the reaction Mila had had—which, by the look on her face, annoyed her more than a little.

"Oh, hello, sir." Danica almost bowed, but stopped herself and instead held out a hand to shake. "I'm Danica Meadows, Mila's roommate. I suspect she's already told you that." Her smile was wooden as she turned to Mila. "So, where exactly did you meet?"

"I just arrived in town," Finn answered instead, "and am in a similar line of work as Mila. So we decided to team up for a bit." He shook Danica's hand.

This not being the first time he'd had to twist the truth to fit the situation in a pinch, he thought that one was pretty good.

"Oh. Well, that's just grand. Perchance, will you be stopping by the house later?" Danica seemed to be having a slight meltdown since her voice had risen in tone and speed.

"What the hell is wrong with you?" Mila asked, cocking her head and screwing up her face. "Why are you talking like a Victorian all of a sudden?"

"Oh, am I?" Danica seemed to not know what to do with her hands, and eventually put them on her hips in a Wonder Woman pose. "I was just a little nervous meeting your handsome new friend is all."

"Well, stop it. You're freaking me out." Mila shook her head slowly.

"Danica, it's a pleasure to meet you. Trust me when I say there is no need to be nervous. I'm just a traveler. I have no intention of throwing my weight around."

He realized it was an odd thing to say from Mila's point of view, but the relief on Danica's face told him that she had gotten the message. He was not here in the capacity of his royal birth.

Danica deflated visibly and smiled. "That is so good to hear. Where are you traveling from?"

"Canada," Finn said with a smile.

Danica smiled back. "Canada? I wasn't aware there were any… important people in Canada."

Mila's jaw dropped. "Danica! I can't believe you would say something like that."

"No, I understand what she means," Finn assured the small woman, whose temper was rising fast. "Maybe we can talk more at length about that when I see you next?"

"That would be wonderful," Danica said, then looked down the street as the sirens suddenly became very loud.

Three police cars came around the corner, their lights painting the street red and blue. "I should probably get out of here. It's been a long night, and I have to work in the morning. Finn, it was nice to meet you. I hope we can talk more soon."

"Same, Danica." Finn shook her hand again.

Penny stuck out a taloned hand, and without missing a beat, Danica offered her a finger to shake. She then turned and walked down the sidewalk, glancing back only once before crossing to the other side and continuing on.

"I swear that girl is at the same time the most brilliant person I know and the densest." Mila was still shaking her head. "Where are we going, anyway?"

"I want to stop at the market. It should only take half an hour or so." He again led the way down the street.

She fell into step beside him, and they made their way, pointedly not looking at the cops piling out of their cars and into the bar.

CHAPTER TEN

Finn led Mila around the corner and into the alley. It wasn't so narrow that it felt dangerous, but it was narrow enough that no cars drove down it. A few lights lit the corridor, but it was mostly in darkness, which wasn't a problem for Finn and his dark vision. Mila, on the other hand, was hesitant to go down the dark passage with him.

"I thought you wanted to go to the market? This alley doesn't go anywhere like that. I think there's a bodega around the corner," she said, stopping at the mouth of the alley, still in the light of the streetlamps.

"Bodega?" Finn asked, glancing at Penny, who just shrugged.

"Yeah, like a little market. They sell beer and smokes and snacks and stuff? You've never heard of a bodega?" She stopped and held up a finger. "Oh, right. Not from around here. That's going to take a lot of time to get used to."

"Ah, I see. When I said market, I meant a market for my kind of people. A magical market, if you will." Finn smiled and took her hand, leading her down the alley.

"How do you even know where this place is?" Mila protested but followed.

"The elves told me about it."

"You know that sounds insane, right?" She laughed.

Finn frowned. "Does it? It just sounds like a fact to me." He saw a section of brick wall that had a glowing magical script about halfway up, and he knew he had found the right place. "Here we are."

Mila looked left, then right, then gave him a sour face. "This is a blank wall, Finn."

"Only to your forgetful eyes," he said with a wink.

The script read LO-DO Market. He rapped on the brick as if knocking on a door and stood back to wait.

"What does 'lo-do' mean?" he asked while they waited.

"That's the name of this district. It's short for lower downtown. It's pretty small but it's nice. Why?"

Finn pointed at the glowing magical sign. "That's what they call this place. LO-DO Market."

"What are you point—"

She was cut off when a section of brick slid to the side, revealing a black space that was quickly filled by two large catlike eyes.

"What the fuck…" Mila murmured, unconsciously stepping closer to Finn in case she needed to use him as a shield.

The eyes regarded all three of them for a second before rumbling, "Password."

Finn gave a smile and leaned in. "Peabrains are forgetful."

The eyes swiveled back to Mila. "Not Peabrains that ain't been woke."

Finn didn't lose his smile, but ran his hand through his hair and held it up, turning so the eyes could see the markings. "She's with me. I'll keep an eye on her."

"You're a fucking dwarf king?" The rumbling voice sounded a little surprised. "Thought you all died a thousand years ago or sumpin'."

Finn just shook his head. "We're harder to get rid of than you might think."

"Ain't that the fuckin' truth." The big thing sighed. "All right, fine, but keep her on a short leash. Don't want the boss coming down on me."

"If you get any flack, just send him my way." Finn gave the eyes a half-bow.

A sound like gravel tumbling down a mountain came out of the slot. It took Finn a second to understand it was laughter. "I fuckin' will, Your Highness. I fuckin' will. Right. Come on in. Mind your step."

The slot banged closed, and nothing happened.

"What the fuck?" Mila said again, her brow rising. "I thought he was going to open a door or something."

"He will. Probably just needs to get there. He sounded old," Finn said, defending the creature.

Mila cocked her head up at him. "How could you tell?"

Finn shrugged. "I don't know. Just a feeling."

Before she could say more, the wall suddenly started sprouting bubbles.

Mila gasped. "What the hell is that?"

"It's magic," Finn said, pulling out the box of Charleston Chews she'd given him at her office and offering her one. She didn't even seem to notice, but Penny tapped him on the head rather insistently until he handed her one. He

93

tossed a few in his mouth, then put the box away and watched the show.

The bubbles at first seemed to be random, but it soon became apparent that they were forming an arched passage. Quicker and quicker, the bubbles appeared, until they were coming so fast that Finn couldn't follow them. When the last bubble took its place in the arch, the space inside went black as the bricks faded from existence and were replaced by steps leading down. Electric sconces lined the brick walls. A quick glance showed no sign of the large-feline-eyed doorman anywhere.

"Shall we?" Finn offered his arm, and Mila slipped hers into it, her jaw open and her wide eyes blinking slowly.

He led her through the arch and down the first couple of steps.

"Just so you know, this magic is way better than your axe."

Penny snickered, puffing smoke rings in her mirth.

"I didn't want to start you off with the big stuff." Finn gave Penny a sideways look. "Besides, Fragar is a much more powerful bit of magic than this whole passage. Stick with Penny and me long enough, and you'll see some stuff that makes your toes curl."

They descended slowly, letting Mila take in the changes. Finn had seen places like this in his time, but he appreciated the detail the creator had put into it. Each step was like taking a step back in time. The steps started out as regular old concrete, with electric lights on the brick walls. Ten steps later, the floor was covered in tiles that looked like they were from the fifties, and the electric lights dimmed with sconces that looked like they were from the twenties. Every ten steps, the materials and technology changed to some older version, until they were walking down stone steps with flaming torches on the wall.

The last section, however, made Mila gasp.

The steps were still cut stone, though a uniform design, but the wall lights were what held her focus. The sconces were now obviously of a magical nature. Blue wisps of smoke rose from the bright, constant light held in golden cages that floated independent of the wall.

Finn smiled at her reaction. He and Penny were used to this level of casual magic, but he had to admit it would probably freak him out if he had just found out magic was real only an hour or two before.

The opening at the bottom of the steps spilled warm bright light into the stairwell, and then came the sounds of people conducting business. As they stepped off the final step, Mila's eyes were wide and swiveling, trying to look at everything at once.

This was Finn's and Penny's kind of place. Tightly packed booths, along with the smell of grilling meats and spices so exotic they were one of a kind. Finn's dwarven nature told him they were exactly one hundred feet below the surface streets, and the old-style construction of the cavernous room fit with that instinct. The ceiling was a series of arches made of stone and handmade brick, painted white, that soared two stories high. The market filled every corner of the large space, leaving narrow lanes between tents and small wooden booths. Finn could see several tunnels that entered the market, but the staircase seemed to be the only direct way back to the surface.

Then there were the people.

Elves, trolls, goblins, and, surprisingly, Peabrains made up the majority of the customers, but there were plenty of examples of rarer species haggling and selling wares. This was a place where Magicals could be who they were without fear of being discovered, so no one used a concealment spell, giving Mila the full experience.

"This is unbelievable," she said, scanning the bustling crowds. "This has been just a few blocks from my house the entire time?"

"There are usually a few of these in every city. Especially if the city is full of Nonmagicals. Come on, we need to find a Huldu." Finn pulled her into one of the aisles and wove his way through the crowd. He stopped at a booth run by a young-faced wood elf.

She smiled and brushed brown hair over her shoulder. "What can I help you with, sir?" Her smile faltered a little when she realized he was a dwarf. "Oh my. I thought there weren't any more dwarves on Earth. Welcome!"

Finn laid on the charm. "Well, hello there. This is quite the booth you have." He fingered a few dried flowers that hung in bunches. She was selling reagents for potions, and the smell of the fragrant ingredients overpowered even the smells of cooking meats from the street vendors. "I'm pretty new in town and could use a little help. I'm looking for a Huldu to make a deal with."

She grinned. "I can help you out. For a price."

Finn nodded. Turned out, every world worked the same, even the ones lost in space for time immemorial.

"I have a little coin."

The elf glanced at Penny and jutted her chin. "I was

thinking something a little simpler. Maybe some saliva from your faerie dragon friend?"

Penny narrowed her eyes. Spit from a dragon was a powerful reagent, but from a faerie dragon, it was even more so, considering how rare they were. Penny dug one claw into his shoulder, one of their shorthand signs that she agreed, regardless of what her face said. It was a good way to keep negotiations going.

"We can do that, but in exchange, I'll need you to throw in a few healing potions," he said, spying the rack of pre-made stock she had on a small shelf in the back.

"Deal." She quickly grabbed a paper bag and began wrapping test-tube-style vials to keep the glass from clinking together.

"Did you say 'healing potions?'" Mila asked quietly, standing very close to Finn to keep the aisle clear. "Like, you drink it and, what? You just heal?"

"Yeah." He chuckled. "It's like magic."

She rolled her eyes. "You're hilarious."

The elf turned back around, having wrapped four vials and stuffed them in the bag. She produced a small empty glass bottle and handed it to Penny, who took it in her front hands and sat on her haunches. Finn watched the dragon work up a good wad of spit before stuffing her muzzle in the bottle's opening and letting it dribble out.

It was a little gross, and Finn decided he didn't need to watch from such a close distance.

"So, you know where I can find a Huldu?" Finn asked, snapping the elf's attention away from Penny.

"I can do you one better. I'll send a message and have

them come meet you here. Should only take them twenty minutes or so. Their station is close."

"Sounds good."

Penny held out the small stoppered bottle, now half-full of bubbly saliva. The elf reached for it, but Finn grabbed it first.

"I'll take the potions now, and leave the saliva here."

He lifted the bottle over his head and, with his finger, drew a few quick runes that glowed softly with purple magic. He set the bottle down, and there was a very dim flash of purple light from under it.

"I've sealed the bottle to the table. As soon as the Huldu show up, I'll release it. Insurance, you understand."

The elf woman gave him a sly smile. "I can live with that. Come back in twenty minutes. I'm sure the Huldu will want to talk to you."

Finn held up the paper bag in salute. "Pleasure doing business with you. See you in a bit."

He led Mila away from the booth and moved deeper into the market.

"What was that?" Mila asked. "The thing you did with the bottle."

"Oh, that's just a simple holding spell. It's called rune magic. Only dwarves practice it. It has varying degrees of potency, all based on handwriting, and the amount of energy the writer channels into the glyph."

"So that bottle will just stay stuck to the table until you release it?" She glanced to their right and saw a stall selling roasting meat on a stick.

"No, I didn't really power that one all that much. It was more of a formality. I'm guessing the magic will wear off in about twenty or thirty minutes. That whole thing was for later interactions with her." He shook the bag with the healing potions in it. "Her potions looked particularly good, and if I'm honest, I can go through quite a few of them. It would be good to have a dealer I can trust."

"Can we get some of that?" She pointed at the meat on a stick. "It smells amazing."

Penny clapped her hands excitedly. "Chi, chi!"

"I know you're hungry, Penny. You're always hungry." He laughed and turned toward the stand. "Sure, let's do it. I could stand to eat as well."

The person tending the cart was a tall, gray-skinned mountain troll with short tusks protruding from his bottom lip and continuing just past his top lip.

"A fuckin' dwarf. Didn't we wipe you out? I thought all you bastards were dead ages ago," he rumbled in a gravelly voice.

"I've been getting that a lot lately," Finn joked, not rising to the bait. "I'm neutral in the whole conflict. Too much to do to worry about who said what to who a few thousand years ago. Today, I would just like to purchase some of your delicious meats. My friend here has never had Skak, and I said yours was some of the best smelling seasoning I've ever come across."

The troll stood a little straighter and showed a flicker of a smile. "It's me dear ol' gran's recipe. Brought it all the way from the old world, she did."

"Well, it smells delicious. How much can I get for a half-Thul?" Finn asked, tucking the bag of potions in his jacket pocket with one hand and fishing in his pants pocket with the other.

He pulled out a small handful of silver balls of various sizes, each with a tiny runes stamped into them. He fished out a medium-sized ball and held it out.

The troll's eyebrows rose, and he reached out to grasp the dense metal in his meaty fingers. "I haven't seen a Thul in ages. My great-grandfather had some that were passed down to him, but the family sold them ages ago. You know we don't use these for money anymore. Where the fuck you from, dwarf?"

"Oh, I just have a pretty good stash that my family kept," Finn said, backpedaling. "What do you take, then?"

The troll shrugged. "Local currency, mostly. Bartering when it's an unusual item."

"Oh, well. I don't have any local currency. Just got into town, you know how it goes."

The troll nodded. "It's fine. I'll take it. Mind you, this is worth quite a bit, so pick whatever you want." He waved a hand over the cart and its many selections.

"Excellent! Ladies? What will you have?" Finn glanced at Penny and Mila. Mila was staring at the troll and not paying attention.

Penny, on the other hand, was on it. Her taloned pointer finger began jabbing at different cuts. "Chi, chi, shrip, shir, chi…" She tapped her chin thoughtfully for a second. "Chi, shi."

The troll most likely hadn't understood her words, but her finger had done most of the talking, and he quickly piled her selections into a paper basket and handed it to Finn.

"Tell you what, just give Mila and me a couple of your

favorites. Can't go wrong with the cook's selections, I always say."

The troll smiled, revealing yellow teeth, and began piling up two more paper baskets. Finn thanked him, and they found a small area set up with tables for patrons of the several food carts in the vicinity. They sat down next to a couple of witches, who were leaning together and looking at a phone and laughing.

Mila seemed to be coping pretty well, all things considered. She glanced around at the tables full of various races that, up until an hour ago, she had thought were nothing but the works of fantasy writers.

Finn took a bite of the juicy meat, letting the exotic spices linger while he slowly chewed. Skak was one of his favorite street foods, and it was pretty hard for him to find, considering it was traditionally a troll food.

"What was the deal with that troll, by the way? He didn't seem to like you very much at first." Mila asked, taking a bite, her eyes going wide as a moan of pleasure hummed out of her. "Holy shit, this is amazing." She stopped chewing, and a look of horror crossed her face. "This isn't, like, rat or something gross, is it?"

Finn laughed. "No, it's beef. Well, the one you're holding is. That one is lamb, and that one is buffalo."

"Good. I would hate to suddenly become addicted to rat. That's not something you can easily explain to your friends." She took another bite and rolled her eyes in pleasure. "This is so good. It's like if curry and fried finger steaks had a baby, then that baby figured out soy sauce."

Penny was nearly halfway through her basket, and showing no signs of stopping. Finn knew a few of his skewers were going to disappear to her sneaky fingers before they were done.

"To answer your first question, us dwarves and trolls haven't exactly seen eye to eye for a very long time." He took another bite and thought about how to put it best. "A misunderstanding happened a long time ago, and it sort of turned into a war. It's been going on for a few thousand years, and it makes things a little dicey when we interact. I've declared myself neutral, and have no intention of keeping the stupid conflict going. At this point, though, it's nearly ingrained in all dwarves and trolls from birth."

"You seemed to handle that pretty well back there. I thought he was going to kick you out at first."

Finn shrugged. "I've had to get good at smoothing over hostile interactions. Being a dwarf can be a hassle when dealing with other races."

"Yeah, but being a prince probably helps quite a bit." Mila smiled, finishing a skewer and moving on to the next.

Finn sighed. "You would think so, but usually, it just means I have a bigger target on my back."

CHAPTER ELEVEN

Twenty minutes and several meat skewers later, they made their way back toward the elf's booth.

"What is a Huldu, exactly?" Mila asked. Now that she had some food in her, she seemed to be taking the whole experience in stride, which impressed Finn quite a bit.

"They're gnomes."

"Gnomes? Like, the little guys with the red hats?" Mila cocked her head.

"What? No. Well, I guess they could wear red hats, but they aren't particularly known for that. The Huldu are the mechanics of the ship. They take care of all the systems, but especially the engines."

Mila's disbelief was written across her face. "Earth has engines?"

"Yeah. Organicum Industria Core engines. They were the most powerful engines ever created and were the catalyst for the design and construction of the terrestrial-class supercruisers like *Earth*. Very expensive, though, so only six were ever made." He pointed down the aisle. "Looks like our elf friend came through for us."

Standing beside the booth with the elf woman were two short, old-looking men with rather large heads. They had on brown jumpsuits that looked like they had been covered in grease, then washed in more grease. They were talking to each other excitedly and didn't see them approaching.

Finn stepped up and towered over both of them. Mila was about the same height, maybe an inch or two shorter, but her confidence had returned after their meal in this alien place, and she naturally adopted a power pose that gave her gravitas. The two gnomes took a step back at the sudden appearance, then their eyes went wide.

"Holy shit. You really *are* a dwarf!" the first one said.

The second leaned to the side and looked up at his rune tattoos. "And a royal to boot."

The first smiled, showing bright white teeth that contrasted with his grease-stained skin. He put out a hand. "I'm Garret, and this is my partner Hermin. Boy, are we glad to see you."

"Hello, Garret. Hermin." He shook both hands, giving them nods. "I'm Finnegan, and this is my partner Penny. This lovely young woman is Mila. It's a pleasure to meet a couple of the fellows who have kept this beast running well past her decommission date. Well done, sirs."

The two gnomes looked at one another, then Hermin spoke up. "Well, 'running' is a relative term. The Elemental fixed her up for now, but the work is never really done. Speaking of, if you're here on *Earth*, that means you have a ship, right?"

Finn waggled his hand. "Sort of. I have one, but it

crashed, and I need some parts to get her running again. That's what I wanted to talk to you about."

He dug the list of parts from his pants pocket and handed it to Garret. Both Huldu leaned in and read down the list.

Garret began nodding. "I think we can get you what you need. You're flying an asteroid-class, then?"

"Yeah, it's pretty bare-bones, but the ol' *Anthem* gets the job done. Mostly," he added, considering the ship was currently in pieces on the side of a mountain.

"It'll take us a few days to get the parts, and they won't come cheap." Hermin's eyes twinkled. "We have a leaking magma valve under Yellowstone that we need to shut off soon, or the whole thing might blow again." That made Mila stiffen, and Hermin waved away her concern. "Don't worry, lass. We can contain it if we need to, but it's going to be a hell of a job. If we had one of those handy dwarven artifacts to protect us, it would make the job a whole lot easier."

Finn frowned. "Aren't the truly powerful artifacts still in storage?"

Garret and Hermin both barked a laugh. "Those were raided and emptied out long ago," Hermin explained. "A faction of us decided they knew better and tried to take things into their own hands. They call themselves the Kashgar, the tall bastards." It sounded like the "tall" in "tall bastards" was more the curse than the other way around.

"Kashgar?" Finn raised an eyebrow. He had never heard of such a group.

"Yeah," Garret took up the narrative. "They rebelled and cocked up the whole works. They've changed their appearance enough that they look more or less like Peabrains. They've infiltrated everything up on the surface, always looking for a way to get back home. We told 'em this was our home now. The war has settled down, now that the Elemental shook things up, but mark my words, it won't be long before we see them cockin' things up again."

"I'll be sure to keep an eye out," Finn reassured them.

"See that you do. If they get wind there's a ship on *Earth*, they'll stop at nothing to steal it," Hermin said, smacking a fist into his palm. "The tall bastards."

"So, what artifact are you looking for in particular?" Finn asked, getting them back on track. "And why do you need me to find it? Can't you locate it?"

"You know how hard it is for anyone but a dwarf to find dwarven artifacts." Garret frowned at him as if Finn were particularly dense. "You people run a different kind of energy than the rest of us. We could find it, but it would be more trouble than it's worth, and it would probably be too late by then anyway."

Hermin waved the argument away. "We're looking for the Helm of Awe."

Finn's brows rose. "One of Fafnir's creations? That's the one that makes you invulnerable to everything for an hour, right? You guys aren't messing around. Okay, I can locate it for you. What do you say we meet back here in three days?"

"You think you can find it in three days?" Hermin sounded doubtful.

"I can find anything in three days," Finn smirked. "Procuring it might be a problem, but leave that to me. Hopefully, it's just buried and forgotten somewhere, and I can dig it up, no fuss. Either way, I'll have something for you by then."

They all shook hands, and the Huldu were about to leave when Finn remembered the whole reason he and Mila were here together. "Hey, guys. Could you tell me one more thing?"

The Huldu turned back, and Hermin nodded. "If we know."

"Have either of you heard of a group going by the name 'the Dark Star?'" Finn pulled the picture of Jeff and Mila out of his pocket. "They took a friend of ours, and we're hoping to get some info on his whereabouts."

The two gnomes took the photo and looked at it, but Finn noticed the elf woman in her stall next to them stiffen at the name.

"I've heard the name mentioned a few times, but we don't spend much time above ground. But this guy," Hermin pointed to the picture, "we've talked to on a number of occasions. Jeff would find us the occasional dwarven-made artifact when we were in a tight spot. He wasn't very good at it, but better than most. And he had the ability to use most of them, which is rare if a dwarf doesn't pass on the right words. When did he go missing?"

"About a week ago," Mila said.

"Well, I'll do what digging I can, but like I said, we spend most of our time underground." He handed back the photo. "We'll see you in three days."

Finn nodded and turned to talk to the elf, but she was gone.

"What's wrong?" Mila asked when she saw him lean into the booth and look around.

"That elf seemed to know who this Dark Star is, or she'd at least had heard the name. She reacted when I said it to the Huldu." Finn frowned, then pulled out the box of chews and popped one in his mouth. He handed a second one to Penny without even looking, and she cooed her appreciation.

"Maybe we can catch her in three days." Mila stifled a yawn. "I don't know about you, but I am beat. I need to sleep, or I'm going to pass out. I don't suppose you have a place to stay?"

"I can find a hotel or something." Finn smiled and waved her concern away.

She huffed and took him by the arm, heading for the exit. "Not without any money, you can't. Come on, you two can stay on my couch."

They headed out of the market and back up to the surface streets. The night had progressed without them, and it was well into the three o'clock hour by the time they passed the Refinery, its lights out and doors locked up. Even the cops were gone.

They walked in silence for a bit, weaving their way block by block back to the alley where she had parked her Hellcat. As they waited for the light to change on Market Street and a few cars to pass, Penny asked a question.

"Chee shiri que. Qui ches?" She was riding Finn's shoulder closest to Mila and had directed the question to her.

"I'm sorry, Penny. I don't understand," Mila apologized.

Finn chuckled softly. "It's quite all right. Faerie Dragon is a pretty difficult language to understand. It took me years to be fluent, and I was raised learning draconic languages. She said, 'you have research computers here on *Earth*. Do you have one at your home?'. She wants to do some background research for the Helm of Awe. That's usually how we start a search."

They crossed the street and turned right while Mila tried to understand the request.

"Like the internet?"

Finn and Penny shrugged at the same time. "I suppose. Is this internet some kind of database?"

"Yeah, it's... well, it's everything. If it's been written or talked about, there's probably something somewhere on there about it. But you'll have to dig for the really rare stuff. You can use my laptop. I'll set you up when we get inside." She pointed to a set of glass doors on the last building on the block and pulled out her keys.

With a practiced hand, she turned the lock and opened the door for them in one smooth movement. They followed her into a small lobby with mailboxes on the wall and a small table with a vase of flowers in its center. A staircase wrapped around a small elevator, and there was a door marked 101, and one marked 102, cater-cornered from one another. Mila pressed the button for the elevator, and the doors opened immediately.

They walked in, and she pressed the button for the fourth floor. The doors closed with a *ding*, and the car began a slow but steady climb.

"I don't know why they installed such a slow elevator in this building. They rebuilt the whole thing from the ground up only ten years ago. For as much as I spent on this place, you would think they could have put out for a good elevator," Mila complained, clutching her key a little tightly.

Finn could tell she was nervous about letting him and Penny into her place, and he couldn't blame her. He decided to try to break the tension.

"Are you okay?"

"Yeah, I'm just worried that Danica will flip out when she sees you sleeping on the couch in the morning," she confessed.

Finn laughed, remembering the awkward conversation he and Danica had had on the street. "I think she'll be fine. She seems like a smart girl who would be hard-pressed to be truly shocked."

Mila laughed. "I hope you're right."

The elevator opened, and Finn saw there were only two units on this level as well. On one side was 402, but Mila went to the other, marked 404, and inserted her key.

The place was pretty big and felt even more so with the lack of walls. Everything, from the ceiling to the floors, was made of rich, golden-colored wood, giving the open warehouse a warm, inviting feel. The kitchen with its large dark-granite-topped island flowed directly into a large, open living room with a deep L-shaped couch and a large TV on a stand. Finn could also see some sort of office area with built-in desk and bookshelves. The front wall was floor-to-ceiling windows with a wraparound balcony that looked out on the baseball stadium a few blocks over.

"Wow. This place is really nice," Finn admired, running his fingers over the polished granite counter.

"Yeah, I know." Mila gave a half-smile of pride, looking around her condo. "This and my car are the only things I spend money on. Even then, I need a roommate to help pay the mortgage, so I can save a little each month. This city is murder for housing. Come on, I'll show you the computer and teach you how to get on the internet."

She took them to the office nook and woke her laptop, then opened the browser. She explained the concept of websites quickly, and how to use Google, then went to get Finn some bedding.

"What do you think?" Finn asked Penny once Mila had walked through one of the several doors along one wall.

"Chi shir?"

Finn gave her a sour look. "About her, dummy. This place, all of it."

Penny considered for a second, then gave a sharp nod and shot a smoke ring from her nostril.

"Yeah, I like her too," Finn agreed. "She took the market way better than I thought she would. Just admit it, it's fate."

Penny rolled her eyes, and instead of answering, began slowly typing into the search bar.

"Here are some blankets and pillows," Mila said, making Finn turn and head her way. "I didn't know if Penny needed her own or not, so I just brought two of each."

"That's perfect, thank you." He took the folded blankets, and she dropped the pillows on the couch.

"Okay, well, that door there is for the bathroom. If you want a shower in the morning, you can use mine when I'm done. I usually get up by seven, but I have a feeling I'll be sleeping in a little after our late night. I already emailed my boss and told him I'll be off the next couple of days, so no worries there. If there's nothing else, I'll see you in the morning. Oh, and feel free to help yourself to anything in the fridge. Not that there's much in there." She stifled a yawn and headed to her room. "Night." She gave a wave then closed her door.

Finn laid out one of the blankets on the long part of the couch and made a nice little nest out of the other on the short end for Penny. He tossed both pillows to his side and began taking off his boots.

"You going to be on there for a while, or are you going to sleep first?" he asked Penny, who was getting the hang of the computer fairly quickly, and her tapping talons became faster with each passing second.

"Shee tirp," she said without taking her eyes off the screen.

"Okay, well, wake me if anything happens." He dropped his jacket on the chair beside the couch, followed by his harness and black shirt.

"Cirri?" She looked over her shoulder just so he could see the bewildered look on her face.

"I don't know," he said defensively, unbuckling his pants and stripping down to his boxer briefs. "Anything. I didn't like the look that elf had when I mentioned the Dark Star. It's got me a little jumpy." He slipped under the blanket and fluffed the pillows. "Aw, man. Can you get the lights? I think it was that switch there." He pointed to the one beside the door.

Penny huffed but took off. She swooped through the open space and slapped the switch, plunging the condo into relative darkness. The lights of the city sill shone in through the large windows, but it was a calming, warm light that reminded Finn of being out among the stars.

Suddenly, a bright sliver of light cut across the room, making Finn sit up and look toward the kitchen.

The refrigerator door was cracked open and a dragon butt was hanging out of it.

Finn rolled his eyes and flopped back down onto the pillow.

Some things were the same, whether he was in space or on *Earth*. Penny's stomach was one of them.

CHAPTER TWELVE

Mila stripped down to her gray t-shirt and panties before washing her face and brushing her teeth. She thought about getting in a quick shower after spending all day in the dirt, but she was too tired to even contemplate it, so she just washed her face quickly and climbed into bed.

She started to think about how insane things had gotten when she stopped for gas like she had a thousand times before, but before her mind could really get going, she was out, the sweet darkness taking her before she even knew it had happened.

Her dreams were odd, to say the least. First of all, she immediately knew they were dreams, which never happened to her. Usually, she would toss and turn until she woke up wondering why she was scared of a pair of underwear chasing her through her old high school, but at the time, it seemed like the most threatening thing in the world.

This dream, though, wasn't so much surreal as it was just plain confusing. All the people on Earth stood shoulder to shoulder in a line that disappeared into a shapeless, black void. They all seemed to be frozen except her. She walked along the line and saw people of every nationality, and when those were done, she began to see people of different races. Elves, trolls, ents, goblins; you name it, there was a representative in line. She walked and walked, the line of people never-ending and never the same person twice. She couldn't understand what was happening, then she nearly jumped out of her skin when one person stepped forward.

It was a human woman with dark hair and a police badge on her hip. The woman looked around, smiled at her, and motioned for Mila to follow. The woman began to be surrounded by bubbles, and just when Mila thought the bubbles couldn't get any thicker, the whole mess disappeared with a *pop*, taking the woman with them.

"What the hell?"

Mila was very confused and looked up and down the line for some sort of clarification. She saw another person far down the line step forward. Within seconds, they too were surrounded by bubbles and popped from existence. The same happened with another person.

She got the feeling that it was happening all down the line. Not a common occurrence, but not exactly rare, either.

A fluttering on her cheeks distracted her, and she swiped at the sensation, but there was nothing there. Then her other cheek was tickled.

The odd world around her began to fade as the dream receded. With each new flutter on her skin, she woke up more and more, until she was pulled from the dream altogether, and she sat up in bed, sucking in a breath.

She blinked and was trying to figure out what was happening when she caught a fluttering movement in the dark. Reaching over, she turned on the bedside lamp and saw that a large moth had flown in through her window.

Most people wouldn't think it odd that a moth was in their room if they left the window open, but Mila was not most people. She and bugs had a special relationship. They didn't come into her house, and she didn't mess with them. It was a deal they had made when she was too young to understand how odd it was to make deals with bugs, but they had listened. From that day forward, she had done her best to not disturb them, and she had never seen anything, not even an ant, in any home she had ever lived in.

So seeing a moth in her room made the hairs on her neck stand on end. Not to mention having one wake her out of a dead sleep.

The large bug fluttered toward her door, beckoning her to follow.

Mila raised an eyebrow, then slowly reached under her bed and found the handle of the cricket bat she kept under there and pulled it out. Cricket was an awful sport, in Mila's opinion, but its equipment made for an amazing weapon.

She hefted the bat onto her shoulder, edge side out, and slipped out of bed, her bare feet not making a sound on the wooden floor. She crept to the door and listened. She heard light snoring and occasional spates of rapid taps. It took her a second to realize was Penny typing on her laptop.

Mila gave the moth a look like, "What the hell, dude?" but it just flapped its wings more urgently.

She sighed and quietly opened her door, slipping out into the living room. The clock on the wall said it was a quarter to five, and she nearly groaned when she realized she had only been asleep for an hour or so.

She saw the still form of Finn sprawled on the couch, one leg and his bare chest uncovered by the blanket as he snored lightly. Then she saw the nest he had built for Penny, which made her say, "Aw," and pout her bottom lip.

The sound made Penny spin from the keyboard and look at her. "Shrii?" She opened her wings, and with two quick pumps, flew over and landed on the back of the couch in front of Mila. She took in the bat and quickly looked around the room for a threat. "Chi, chir?"

"I don't know what's up. A moth just woke me from a dead sleep and wanted me to check on something out here," Mila said, not exactly understanding Penny, but getting the drift.

Penny cocked her head and raised a questioning eyebrow.

Mila shrugged. "It's complicated. But the only thing I can think is that something was trying to hurt me. Maybe it mistook you two as intruders? That doesn't make sense, though. I've had lots of people here, and this has never happened before."

"Squeeee?" Penny gave her a knowing look.

Mila rolled her eyes. "Not, like, an inordinate amount, but a few. A girl has needs."

Penny smiled and was about to say something when the front door burst open and four guys in black with masks on came pouring in.

Mila screamed and raised the bat, but before she could take a step toward the intruders, Finn was awake and leaping over the couch.

In three bounds, he was upon them.

The first guy had no clue what happened when Finn's rock-hard fist slammed into his face and drove him to the floor in an unconscious heap. The second guy was lifted into the air as Finn slammed a knee into his groin, then punched him in the chest, making the guy wheeze as he slammed into a wooden pillar and cracked his head.

The other two were a little quicker on the uptake and spread out to attack from both sides. With a flick of their wrists, they deployed foldable batons like riot police carried.

Mila saw that Finn didn't hesitate to charge the one closest to the door. The intruder behind him charged right after, his baton raised and aimed at the dwarf's head.

Mila was on the guy before he had a chance to swing, and her cricket bat vibrated in her hands as it made contact with the back of the guy's head, sending him to the ground, completely limp.

Finn had the third guy in a headlock, his arms clamping down with bulging muscles. Mila took a step back at the intensity on Finn's face. Where he was normally all smiles, he had transformed into a beast. His teeth were bared, and foam had gathered at the corner of his mouth. His eyes were nearly gray instead of their normal brown. For the first time, Mila was actually frightened of the man.

Penny swooped past her and landed on Finn's bulging shoulder. She pressed her head to his and began to hum lightly. Immediately, the rage in Finn began to diminish. A light blue glow surrounded Penny, and the effect was even greater. Within seconds, Finn let go of the intruder, who was out cold, and reached a gentle hand up to pat Penny on the back.

"Thanks, friend," he said hoarsely. "That was a hell of a way to wake up."

"Oh, my God," Danica said, sliding to a halt beside Mila. Her eyes were wide, and she was clutching at the hem of her overly large t-shirt. "You're a berserker? What the fuck, dude"

"What the hell does that mean?" Mila asked. "And how the hell do you know what a berserker is? And who the fuck are these guys?"

Mila's head was spinning.

"It's okay," Finn said, standing up and going to the kitchen, opening drawers at random. "It just means I can get a little carried away if I'm not careful. Waking from a full sleep and jumping directly into battle can get my blood pumping a little too fast is all. Do you have any rope?"

"There's some duct tape in the second drawer," Danica said helpfully. Then she turned to Mila. "I know Finn took you to the market last night. So there's something I need to show you."

Finn pulled the drawer open and pulled out the roll. "Perfect." He proceeded to tape the intruders' legs and arms together, then taped them all together, their backs touching. "Go on, Danica. She's a big girl. You should have seen how she handled seeing the troll who sold us Skak."

"Duncan?" Danica grinned and looked into the distance longingly. "His gran's recipe is the best."

Mila held up her hand, trying to slow things down. "Wait, you know about the market?" She stared at Danica for a long second. "Oh. My. God. You're a Magical?"

Danica nodded.

"Wait, don't tell me."

Mila wanted to guess. Her best friend and roommate wasn't even human, and she'd never noticed. But now that she had seen the other races without the concealment spells, she kind of understood how they worked. Thinking back to the times she and Jeff had worked together, and then meeting Duncan, she could see how it didn't really change the person, but the way others perceived them.

Danica was tall, blonde, and one of the kindest people she had ever met. She was a doctor at the children's hospital and had a knack for saving the unsavable. She could be a little slow on the uptake sometimes, but it was endearing rather than a flaw. The fact that she was a high-cheekboned model type was really only the fourth or fifth most remarkable thing about her.

Mila shook her head in bewilderment. "The more I think about it, the more I wonder how I didn't figure this out sooner. You have got to be an elf, right?"

Danica smiled so brilliantly Mila thought she might start dancing. "Yup. Oh, man, I hated not telling you, but most Peabrains lose their shit when they hear about Magicals."

"Can I see you without your spell?" Mila asked, a little embarrassed, not knowing what the proper etiquette was.

"I already dropped it."

Mila frowned, not seeing any difference. Then she saw the tips of her friend's ears sticking out from her hair and smiled.

"That's so fucking cool."

Danica struck a power pose that was only slightly affected by her t-shirt and socks. "Thanks."

"We have a lot of talking to do, but first, who the fuck are these guys?" Mila asked.

"Kashgar, but that doesn't really mean anything. We need to know who they work for," Danica said, giving Mila a guilty smile.

"Okay, I feel like I woke up in an opposite world. Usually, I'm the one telling you what's going on." She turned to Finn, who was lightly smacking one of the guys, trying to wake him up. "What are we going to do with them?" she asked him.

"Call the cops, they can handle it from here. The wait for them will give me just enough time to ask our friends here a few questions." Finn smiled when the guy he had been smacking snapped awake. "Oh, hello there, Mr. Kashgar. I have some questions for you."

"Fuck off. I ain't talking," he spat.

Finn ripped the guy's mask off and tore it in half in one quick motion, making the guy's eyes go wide.

Satisfied with the response, Finn leaned in. "Did the Dark Star send you?"

The guy stiffened but said nothing.

"Are they after my ship? Or is it something else?"

Again, the guy said nothing, but panic was beginning to build in his eyes.

"Where can I find this Dark Star?" Finn growled, showing teeth.

The guy opened his mouth, but his entire head was suddenly engulfed in a large bubble, along with his three friends. He began to scream, then the bubble popped, and he just blinked dumbly, looking around as if he didn't know where he was.

Finn sighed and stood up. "Okay, pretty sure it's this Dark Star person. Probably after my ship. We should go check to make sure it's still cloaked. Those old rune sticks weren't the best."

Penny scoffed but agreed with a toot of smoke.

Mila felt like the world had gone crazy. She looked at Danica, who was on the phone with the cops, then at Finn standing in her kitchen over four seemingly clueless people who had just broken into her house.

"Okay, I'm going to put on some coffee. Anyone want any?" Mila said, not knowing what else to do.

"Coffee sounds great." Finn nodded, scratching his six-pack abs, and watching over the intruders.

"Uh, Finn? Would you mind at least putting on some pants? Not that I don't like the show, but the cops might feel a little better if you're not naked when they get here." Mila smiled politely, trying not to look at every inch of him.

"I have underwear on," he protested, snapping the band of the skin-tight shorts.

Mila swallowed. "I'm not sure that it counts when your, uh, outline is still visible."

Finn smiled and turned a little red before going and pulling his jeans on.

Mila made coffee, but she didn't remember doing it. Her mind was full of images of fighting and nearly naked men.

CHAPTER THIRTEEN

Finn gave his statement, and Mila filed the police report, while Danica handed out cups of coffee to everyone. The four bewildered Kashgar intruders were carted off in a paddy wagon, and an hour and a half later, the condo was finally quiet once again.

By that time, the sun was coming up, and it seemed that sleep was just not going to be happening for anyone. Danica made her apologies, explaining she had to get to the hospital. Her first patients were scheduled at eight, and she would be useless until she had a proper breakfast at her regular diner. She promised that she would have a sit-down and talk things over with Mila when she got off her shift.

"Can we switch cars for the day?" Mila asked when Danica came out of her room dressed in black slacks and a conservative white blouse.

Finn noted she still wore black high heels, and he wondered how she could spend the whole day in them.

"Sure, I love driving the beast," she said, dropping her

keys on the counter and taking Mila's from the hook by the door. "You planning on going into the hills?"

"Yeah, we need to check on something for Finn." Mila walked over to her tall, blonde friend and gave her a hug. "Thanks for helping with the cops."

Danica smiled and hugged her friend back with one arm, the other holding her big, black, leather purse. "It was nothing. I just got everyone coffee."

"You also kept everyone calm and happy." Mila pulled back. "Thanks."

Danica patted her on the arm. "No problem. We'll chat tonight. I have patients to see and pancakes to eat! Have fun, you two. Don't do anything I wouldn't." She winked and walked out the door.

"I like her," Finn stated, taking the last sip of his coffee. "You ready to go?"

"Sure, let me just put on my hiking boots and grab a jacket."

Twenty minutes later, they were cruising down the highway in Danica's Subaru Forester. The car was filled with various camping and climbing gear from her and Mila's frequent trips into the mountains. Mila passed the Kum & Go where she and Finn had first met and continued driving.

Finn pointed out the fire road he had traveled down, and Mila turned onto it, slowing the car so they wouldn't kick up too many rocks. After another twenty minutes of climbing the hills, Finn motioned for her to stop.

"It's down there. Is there an easy way to drive down?" he asked.

Mila bit her lip, looking as far up the road as she could see. "I'm not sure. Not many people use this road. I'm not even sure where it goes. It looks like there might be a pullout up ahead, though. We can park there and walk the rest of the way."

"Cher squee?" Penny said, puffing a short flame and a smoke ring.

"Good idea."

Finn found the button to roll down the window, and Penny gave them both a salute before flapping her wings and shooting out of the car and into the air.

"She's going to go ahead and do some scouting. She set the spell markers, so she should have an easier time finding them."

Mila put the car in drive and continued the slow climb. "You really trust her for everything, don't you?"

"She's my partner. Fifty-fifty. I wasn't kidding when I said she was the smartest person I know. That little dragon has gotten me out of more trouble than I care to imagine." He chuckled. "That's not to say she doesn't have a hot head of her own. It's just that her buttons are different than mine. Makes us a good team. We can watch out for one another."

Mila nodded and navigated a tight turn. "Must be nice having someone there for you like that."

"It is," he agreed. "Speaking of being my partner, she found something last night on this internet thing. There was a big discovery in Norway a few months ago, and she saw a picture with the helm in it. But she couldn't find out where it was taken. Do you think you could call around to some of your people in the business and see where it is?"

"Sure. I think I know what site she's talking about. Jeff was going on about it before he disappeared. I'll make the call when we get to your ship thing."

She came around a corner, and there was a pullout for two or three cars. She maneuvered the Forester around so it was facing the way they had come, then shut it off.

"Okay, big guy. Lead the way." She zipped up her fleece vest and slipped her phone in the pocket of her black workout leggings.

Finn cut the trail, using his large size to push branches or ground cover out of the way for Mila's small frame. It took them nearly half an hour to clear the trees to the valley below, where the ship rested inside its cloaking spell.

"So, there's a spell hiding the whole ship? It must be pretty small, then." Mila huffed, jumping across the gap in two boulders.

"It's an asteroid. Probably five hundred feet across," Finn said, offering her his hand to jump down onto the grass below.

"That's crazy big! And you just happened to have a spell to cover the whole thing?"

"Well, Penny had it made special for us a few years ago after we almost got killed by a group of cannibals. The ship had been overrun with locals trying to get inside. It was a whole mess. This way, we can come in and out, and no one knows any better."

Mila frowned, and they walked another few hundred yards down the valley. "I feel like your life is a little too exciting sometimes."

"Me too. That's why we wanted to find the *Earth* and retire off her riches. We're here, by the way." He stopped at what appeared to be an open meadow.

"I don't see anything." She looked left and right, her brow rising.

Finn laughed. "Well, it would be a pretty crap cloaking spell if you could. Come on." He took her hand and walked forward.

Her eyes widened when he started to disappear, as if walking into an invisible wall. She resisted, but he pulled her through in one tug.

She let out a gasp when the *Anthem* suddenly appeared in all her burnt and rocky glory. The amazement faded rather quickly.

"It looks like a big rock."

"It is a big rock. She's an asteroid, like I said."

Penny zipped over, landed on his shoulder, and began a rather complicated series of squeaks and toots, which Finn followed perfectly. He saw Mila looking out of sorts, so he began translating for her.

"She says the area is still untouched, and the cloak is holding up just fine. The reactor has refilled the power cells, but other than the life support and simple systems, the rest of the ship is still dead." He turned to Penny. "Well, yeah, it's still dead. We haven't gotten the parts yet. Did you think the spaceship fairy was going to come along and wave a magic wand at her?" Finn rolled his eyes and chuckled.

Penny didn't seem to find it funny and hopped off his shoulder and onto Mila's. Mila jumped at first but laughed when she saw the look of betrayal in Finn's eyes.

"Don't push us women too hard. We outnumber you now."

"Fine, I'm going to get some supplies from the ship. And a change or two of clothes." He walked to the edge of the ship and began to climb down the hole that led to the airlock.

"I don't suppose you have anything of value on that ship? Something you can sell to make a little Earth money? It would make things a lot easier," Mila called after him.

He thought about that and came up with nothing. "Not really. We sold pretty much everything already just to keep her in the sky."

"No precious metals or gems or something? I thought you were treasure hunters."

"Not really. Just a bunch of gold, but that stuff is worthless. I've been using it for soldering and to patch up small leaks," Finn said, at a loss.

"You have gold?" she asked incredulously. "How much?"

Finn shrugged. "I basically have an unlimited supply. I accidentally picked up an artifact a few years back called Draupnir. It was an armband made for a practical joke my ancestor Fafnir played on his brother, a king at the time. Out in space, gold is everywhere and thus pretty worthless, so it was a real middle finger of a gift. Draupnir bonds with whoever puts it on. Every nine days, it creates nine copies of itself. It's a real bitch to own. In a year, it'll fill up a hold with the stupid armbands. We need to just space the stuff, but I can't get rid of it. Every time we throw it out, it shows back up in the hold, shitting gold out all over the place. It's kind of cursed. Why is it worth a lot here?"

Mila blinked stupidly for a few minutes, trying to

process what he was saying. "Yeah, here on Earth, gold is very valuable. You should grab that thing. It's going to come in handy."

Finn nodded. "Okay, that's that problem solved. Make your calls. I'll be out in a few minutes."

He climbed in and pressed his hand to the airlock controls. The door swished open, and he started the pressurization procedure.

"Gold is valuable here?" he said to himself. "Man, this place is weird."

CHAPTER FOURTEEN

Finn filled a leather backpack with some clothes, a few of Penny's more prized hoard items, and the last bottle of his favorite whiskey. It took nearly twenty minutes to traverse the tilted ship from his and Penny's quarters to the main hold.

The large area was empty, as usual, and he had to do some pretty tricky climbing to get to the far end where they kept Draupnir in its own smaller hold. He pressed his hand to the control panel, and the door swished open, spilling an avalanche of identical golden armbands down the slanted floor of the main hold and against the large double doors he had entered through.

"Great," he groaned to himself. "Now I have to dig my way out of this crap, as well."

He pulled himself into the second hold and had to wade through waist-high piles of the stupid armband. He hated the thing, but it seemed like lugging it across the galaxy was finally going to pay off.

He made his way to the center of the large room, where the original Draupnir hung from a hook on a chain dangling from the ceiling. They found that if they left it on the floor, it would fling the copies of itself all over the place when nine more would appear at the bottom of the pile and displace the entire mess violently. Plus, Penny had the idea that if they made it look important, maybe they would get lucky, and some asshole who got on board to rob them might think it was valuable and take it, passing the curse on to them.

So far, no such luck.

After a few swipes at the just-out-of-reach artifact, one of which sent the thing swinging on its long chain, Finn was finally able to leap up and get his hand on it during a backswing. With a little more effort, he pulled himself up, unhooked the gold band, and stuffed it into his backpack with one hand while he held onto the chain with the other.

Sighing, Finn knew the next part was going to suck, but he didn't want to take the long way down. He began to swing on the chain until he felt he had the angle right, and once he was out in the open, let go. He had to twist a bit in the air, but he was able to fall through the door, and hit the floor of the main hold at a pretty good angle, sliding down and plowing into the pile of replica Draupnirs, sending most of the pile blasting away, as if he were a comet and the golden armbands a bunch of dinosaurs.

Smiling at his good end to a bad situation, Finn stomped a few of the soft metal bands into flattened pancakes and stuffed them in the bag as well, then began the difficult journey outside.

Mila hung up the phone and smiled at Penny, who was sitting next to her on the large boulder a few dozen feet outside the cloaking spell. They had an uninterrupted view of the valley and the city beyond, though, during the day, it was just a mishmash of browns and grays with the occasional line of freeway running through it.

"You were right," Mila confirmed, shaking the phone for emphasis. "There was a shipment of Viking artifacts sent to the Royal Ontario Museum, and the helm was part of it. At least, I think it was. My colleague sent a picture. What do you think?"

She enlarged the picture and showed it to Penny, who squinted while scrutinizing the image, then smiled and nodded.

"Shir ti." A smoke ring shot from her nose, a sign Mila was starting to recognize as the equivalent to "yes," or "correct," or "positive," depending on the circumstance.

"Good. There's a slight problem, however." Mila bit her lip, trying to figure out how to explain it. "Finn is going to need a passport, and if he's supposed to be from Canada, it needs to be from there. But I don't know what they look like. Hell, I don't even know the process to getting one."

Penny waved a hand as if it were no big deal, then broke into a long explanation that Mila didn't understand at all, but she felt confident that Penny was not perturbed in the least.

"Let me guess, you can use magic to get around that?"

Penny touched a talon to the tip of her nose and winked.

Mila laughed. "Okay, I'll leave that to you, then. We will need to buy some plane tickets, but we can do that at the airport. I have a feeling this little trick is going to need to be done in person, right?"

Penny nodded and looked toward the cloaking spell's edge for a few seconds before Finn came out, seeming to appear from nowhere. He was carrying an overstuffed backpack and wore an irritated look on his face.

"Chi shiri, squee?" Penny asked, flapping into the air and landing on his shoulder.

"It's not that big a deal, but I couldn't get the inner airlock hatch to close properly. This old girl is falling apart," he lamented, dropping the bag in front of Mila and squatting to open it.

Mila gasped when he pulled out four crushed armbands and a perfectly maintained one of the same design. She had never seen so much gold in all her life, especially so intricately detailed and preserved. The scrollwork was beautiful, but the thickness and perfect attention to detail made it breathtaking.

"Is that it? Why would you crush the others?" she asked, not understanding how one could destroy such beautiful pieces of work.

Finn raised an eyebrow. "Because they wouldn't fit in the bag with all the other stuff. I would have done the same to the original, but it can't be destroyed—at least, not by anything so mundane as my foot." He demonstrated this by throwing it on the ground and stomping on it viciously.

She let out a whimpering scream to see such a beautiful artifact treated in such a way, but cocked her head in confusion when nothing happened to the normally soft metal, except to be pounded into the earth a bit with each stomp.

"Holy shit. Can I touch it?" She reached for the band.

"Sure, just don't put it on, or it will bond to you. Then you won't be able to get rid of it," Finn warned.

Mila lifted the band and inspected it. She hadn't been working with Viking artifacts for long, but she was picking up on their particular quirks and markings quickly. She recognized some of the stylistic flourishes and pointed them out.

"Oh, yeah," Finn said, pulling a purple, glowing stick of what looked like chalk from the bag. "That was sort of Fafnir's signature. He put that little frill on everything. There's even one on Fragar, and that was one of his early works."

"You keep mentioning him. Who was he?" Mila handed the band to Finn, who stuffed it unceremoniously into the bag, along with the four crushed replicas.

"He was my great-great-great-something uncle," Finn explained, waving for her to follow as he headed back toward the ship with the glowing chalk in hand. "He was one of the greatest smiths to ever live. Built countless weapons and armor pieces. Was actually a passenger on *Earth*. I was really hoping to find his workshop, or at least find some of his stuff in storage. If I had to guess, most of the working artifacts here are more than likely his. He really built shit to last."

They came to the curved edge of the *Anthem*, and he held the chalk up to the rough stone surface and began to make an intricate set of runes.

"Wait, you don't mean the Fafnir from Norse legend, do

you?" Mila asked, trying to remember what had happened to him.

"Probably. He was big shit and liked to show off. It wouldn't surprise me if he took over these Norse people."

He added a few more flourishes, creating a mess of lines and sharp edges. He pressed a hand to the symbol and began to speak in a low voice, just soft enough that Mila couldn't make any of it out.

The symbol glowed purple and rapidly grew in intensity with each word. There was a flash, and the symbol disappeared, leaving nothing behind but a wisp of purplish smoke that dissipated on the wind. A strong smell of pine trees filled the air.

"That's done. Okay, let's get back to town. I'm starving."

"What the hell was that?" Mila pointed to where the symbol had been a few seconds ago.

Finn hiked a thumb at the asteroid. "It's a tracking spell in case it gets discovered and taken. Might as well be careful, with these Kashgar and the Dark Star moping about."

"That's...actually smart. Do you think the chances of that are pretty high?" Mila asked, looking back up the valley to where Danica's car was parked, and dreading the hike.

Finn shouldered the backpack and started back up the hill. "Not sure, but better safe than sorry. So, is there a way we can convert this gold into your money? Or do I need to just cut pieces off and use it by weight?"

Mila laughed. "I would love to see you try to pay for a beer with a gold nugget. There are ways to do it, but if we want to exchange it fast, I know a place. They're not going to give you a great rate, but it'll be enough. Plus, if that thing drops more every nine days, a bad rate won't hurt anything."

"What is this exchange place called?"

"Cash For Gold." She smiled at him.

Finn cocked a smile of his own. "Straightforward. I like it."

CHAPTER FIFTEEN

They made their way down the mountain and into the city proper in just over an hour. Traffic was picking up for the lunch rush, so they found themselves parked on 70, inching along at a crawl.

"Why do you all use vehicles? Is there no public transportation?" Finn asked, waving to a small boy who was staring at him from his car seat in the sedan they were slowly passing.

"We have public transport, but it's not the best. I use it for some things, but mostly, I have to go places the train doesn't stop."

Mila hit her left turn signal and accelerated into the next lane, gaining them about twenty feet.

"I understand that, but what about the rest of these people?" he asked. "Surely, a lot of them can take a train."

Finn was used to worlds where living and working was usually done in the same building, or at least within walking distance. This mass of confusion and angry drivers was an odd system to him.

"I'm sure they can, but people are stubborn." She waited as her phone told her to take the next exit, then changed lanes again, moving to the right. "Plus, we get it stuck in our heads that driving is more convenient."

"Sounds like you Peabrains have forgotten more than just your magic." He smiled at her. "You forgot your ability to reason as well."

"You have no idea, Finn," she said seriously, turning onto the exit ramp and gunning it.

Ten minutes later, they were at a place that had a garish sign that said Cash For Gold in flashing neon.

"I think they need to take your info if you want to make an exchange. You don't have an ID, though," Mila said, unbuckling her seatbelt and holding out her hand. "I'll go do this one, but we need to find a way to get you some identification. And I have a feeling we will need to set up some kind of business where gold is not going to raise much suspicion."

Finn felt like he should be a part of the transaction, but he didn't know well enough how this world worked that he could contradict her, so he pulled one of the pancaked bands from his bag and handed it to her.

"Geez, this thing is heavier than it looks." She stared in wonder at the hunk of metal for a few seconds, then nodded and opened the door. "Okay, wish me luck."

"Good luck." Finn was sincere, but wondered why she was going to need luck.

"Chi, chi!" Penny chuffed, a smoke ring rising slowly from the corner of her mouth.

He watched Mila go into the establishment, and was able to see her walk up to the counter through the large front windows. Penny sat on his knee, observing with rapt interest.

The clerk greeted Mila, and they talked for a few seconds before she placed the flattened metal on the counter. The clerk's eyes widened and he slowly picked it up, giving Mila a shocked stare. He weighed the thing with an electronic scale, then took it into the back.

Mila turned and shrugged, giving Finn a slightly confused thumbs-up through the window.

Finn and Penny snickered at her reaction. She was obviously out of her element, but the interaction was so unlike what Finn was used to, he agreed she had made the right call to go in alone.

After about fifteen minutes, the guy came back with an older man at his side. They spoke with Mila for a few minutes, then each of them shook her hand, and he pulled out several banded stacks of cash, and started counting them out. He got to thirty, then put it all in a paper sack. She gave them a wave and walked out the door, glancing left and right before quickly jumping into the driver's seat.

"Okay, I have to say, that went better than I thought it was going to."

She tossed the bag into Finn's lap and started the car, backing out of the parking lot and pulling onto the road. She glanced into the rearview mirror, seeming rather distracted to Finn.

Penny opened the bag, pulled out one of the bound stacks of money, and began counting the bills, her taloned fingers flying. Finn followed her movements and saw that there were twenty-five hundred-dollar bills. He double-checked and confirmed that there were indeed thirty stacks of them. A quick calculation told him a total of seventy-five thousand dollars was in the bag.

Finn frowned at Mila's jittery behavior. "Is this a lot of money?"

Mila barked a laugh that made her eyes go wide with surprise. "Uh, yeah. That's more than most people make in a year. I'm not going to lie, I feel a little odd having that in the car." She eyed the paper bag for a second before turning down Colorado Street.

"Should we store it somewhere?"

Finn wasn't sure how these people dealt with their currency, but he was picking up that it was a little dangerous to have this much on him at once.

"We'll head to my place and put most of it in my safe. I'm assuming we want to head out as soon as possible to find the helm?"

Finn and Penny exchanged a glance, and Penny gave a short nod.

"Yeah, the sooner, the better," Finn translated. "I don't like having the *Anthem* sitting out in the open with only a cloaking spell to hide her."

Mila nodded, stopping at a red light, and glanced in the rearview mirror again, this time squinting and leaning in.

"Do you recognize that van behind us?" she asked.

Finn turned and looked over his shoulder. He saw a white cargo van behind them, and while he didn't recognize the vehicle or the driver, he recognized what it looked like when he was being followed.

"How long have they been following us?"

"Not sure," Mila confessed. "It's a pretty common make

and model, but I swear they were behind us on the freeway when we were coming back from the ship."

The guy in the van's driver seat was doing his best to not make eye contact with Finn, but there was movement from behind the driver, and Finn made out at least one more guy in the back.

Finn turned to the front and scanned the area. There was a park a block up that had a couple of buildings that looked like restrooms or some kind of storage. The area was pretty dead, and the park was empty at this time of day.

He pointed out the park. "Pull in there, and head for the buildings at the back."

"Do you think it's more Kashgar?" she asked, stepping on the gas and flipping on the turn signal.

"Not sure, but I think we're about to find out." He cracked his knuckles and put the bag of money on the floor beside his backpack.

Penny cleared her throat, puffing a few flames in preparation.

"Man, I wish I had my bat," Mila lamented, checking the mirror again. "They're pulling in behind us."

"Park behind the brick building there on the left." He pointed. "Don't want to be seen, if I'm going to be slinging spells around."

Mila hit the gas and sped through the park's winding drive, turning into the parking lot by the restrooms fast enough that the Forester's tires squealed a bit. She slipped into a space, threw the car into park, and unbuckled her seatbelt. To Finn's surprise, she climbed over the seat and started rummaging in the back.

"I'll be right behind you, I think there's something I can use back here." She tossed a pair of shoes and a rolled-up sleeping mat over her shoulder.

Finn stepped out of the car and walked a few paces away, reaching behind his back and wrapping his hand around Fragar's handle, but not pulling it out.

The van squealed into the lot a second later, and the back doors were open before it fully stopped. Four tall guys in jeans and t-shirts piled out, forming a half-circle. They each had a weapon. Finn counted two bats and a knife, and one had a full-on short sword. The driver climbed out slower than the rest, a look of supreme confidence on his face.

Finn sized up each of the men, rating them by threat. The driver, while unarmed, was at the top of the list. Finn had seen his type before—a mage trained in combat spells if his lack of a weapon and surplus of cocksure manner were any indication.

"Finnegan Dragonbender, I presume," the mage sneered, oozing contempt as he flipped his blond hair out of his face. "You have something my lord requires."

"An attitude adjustment?" Finn guessed, causing Penny to chuckle, a roiling flame escaping from the side of her mouth.

The look of rage that flashed over the mage's face was all Finn needed to know exactly what kind of people he was dealing with.

Zealots.

He hated zealots, the irrational bastards.

"The Dark Star suffers no fools," the man growled, taking a step forward, his left hand glowing gold and crackling with energy.

"Suffers you, though? Seems like a conflict of conviction to me."

Finn readied a spell of his own, but he was a lot less obvious about it, keeping his left hand clenched to hide the telltale purple glow of his dwarvish magic. "Before we get to the main event, maybe you could fill me in on who you guys are exactly, and why you follow someone who has the audacity to call themselves 'The Dark Star'—one of the most ridiculous names I've ever heard, by the way."

"We are Her Lady's knights. You have the honor of speaking with Lithor, her First Knight." He took a mock bow. "Her vision is one far too long in the making. She will free us all from this life of secrecy, and establish a nation where those of us who have not forgotten the true arts of magic may live free and out in the open. We will be unstoppable. Finally, an age of—"

"Okay, I get it," Finn interrupted, waving his hands to make the mage stop his monologue. "Fucking zealots," he mumbled to himself, getting an eye roll from Penny. "So, what is it she wants from me?"

Lithor chuckled. "Isn't it obvious? You have the only working ship on this broken-down planet. With such a ship, we would be able to move our plans forward by decades. A magical ship such as yours would let us dominate the skies against the Peabrains' machines of war."

Finn frowned and gave Penny a sidelong look. Penny shrugged, knowing what he was thinking.

"You know the *Anthem* isn't a warship, right? And she's not exactly flightworthy at the moment."

Lithor waved a hand in dismissal. "It matters not. The

ship can be outfitted with weapons, but the core of the ship is something we cannot make with the primitive tools left on this planet. Do yourself a favor, dwarf, and just hand it over. No one needs to get hurt today."

The back door to the Forester opened, and Mila came out, an aluminum walking stick in her hands. She held it like a short spear, and her face was all determination. Finn nearly groaned; he had been hoping she'd stay in the car. If they were looking at a physical fight, she would have been a welcome addition, but with Lithor in the mix, she was now a liability. He would need to protect her.

"Well, well. Look who joined the party," Lithor said, a wicked smile on his face. "It seems a Peabrain has decided to meddle in things she does not understand."

The four Kashgar with weapons began to move, circling around Finn and Mila in careful side steps. They kept their distance, but Finn was sure they could be within striking distance in a flash when they wanted to be.

"What's it going to be, Dragonbender? Hand over the ship, or do we take you and your little friend here and torture it out of you? Better yet, we torture her and make you watch. I'm betting that would get you talking."

Lithor flicked his wrist, and a stream of golden light shot out of his fingertips to wrap around Mila, pinning her arms to her side. A stream of bubbles flowed down the light and began to cling to her. When a bubble popped, she let out a small cry of pain. Lithor turned his grinning face toward Finn, daring him to do anything.

Finn got angry, and not the rational kind of angry, but the berserker kind of angry. A lot of things happened all at once then. In one motion, he pulled Fragar from its holster, whispered the power word, and threw the still unfolding axe at the string of golden light. Penny shot off his shoulder like a bullet, her wings barely flapping. Instead, her magic propelled her right at Lithor's face.

The mage's eyes widened, and he raised a hand to block the little dragon. The four Kashgar charged Finn, their weapons raised and murder in their eyes.

Fragar unfolded and sliced through the magical thread as if it were a simple string. A shockwave ran back along the line and sparked when it hit Lithor's fingers, making him scream in pain. The other half vanished the instant the line was severed, and Mila slumped to the ground and sucked in a deep breath.

Penny dug her claws into Lithor's face, eliciting a scream of pain, and making him fall to the pavement. He held his right eye with his good hand, blood pouring from a gash in his cheek and the eye.

Finn grabbed the arm of the Kashgar with the knife, allowing the two with bats to hit him across the shoulders. His rage let him shrug off the blows with barely a twitch. He pulled the wrist with the knife, making the man stumble forward out of control, and sent him knife-first into the Kashgar behind Finn, who had his short sword raised for a killing blow. The knife sank into the swords-man's chest, making his eyes go wide as he collapsed onto his comrade.

Finn spun to the bat wielder on his left and charged, lifting him in a low tackle and slamming him to the ground, knocking the wind out of his opponent by driving his shoulder deep into the Kashgar's stomach.

He ripped the bat from the downed man's hands and

lifted it to block the downswing of the other bat, but it wasn't there. Instead, he saw Mila slashing the walking pole across the other man's back and shoulders.

He cringed in pain and turned to face Mila, but Finn threw his bat as hard as he could. A crack resounded as the wooden implement slammed into the back of the Kashgar's head and dropped him instantly.

The sound of slamming doors and squealing tires made Finn jump to his feet and get ready to dodge a van, but the vehicle was speeding away from them.

Finn breathed deep, letting the rage subside as best he could to assess the situation. There were only three Kashgar left, the one with the knife and the mage both fleeing the scene without them.

Penny landed on his shoulder and fed some of her calming magic into him, resulting in the smell of spring flowers filling the area and his rage being sucked from him. He took a deep breath, his calm self once again reestablishing control.

"Thanks, friend." He patted Penny's small shoulder, and she tooted a ring of smoke in reply.

Finn turned to see the three remaining Kashgar's heads surrounded in a bubble, which popped, wiping their memories and rendering them useless for interrogation.

"Are you okay?" he called to Mila, who was still in a fighting stance and breathing heavily as she wielded the walking stick like a sword.

She gave a few sharp nods. "Yeah, I'm good. You?"

He gave her a thumbs-up, then slowly climbed to his feet. "We should get out of here before the police show up. These guys won't remember a thing."

"Should we call an ambulance? That guy was stabbed." She pointed the end of her walking stick at one of the guys crumpled on the ground.

"No point," he grunted, leading her back to the car. "He's already dead. But don't worry, he would have happily killed you first."

"That shouldn't make me feel better," she said, falling into the driver's seat after he opened the door for her.

Finn leaned into the open door and gave her a half-grin. "But it does anyway, right?"

Mila bit her lip, then nodded. "Yeah. Let's get the fuck out of here."

CHAPTER SIXTEEN

After a short stop at Mila's condo to lock all but a couple of stacks of bills in her safe, and to change into travel-appropriate clothing, they walked a few blocks to the train and headed for Denver International Airport.

Finn had been worried about leaving Danica alone when the Dark Star's people presumably knew where Mila lived and could come back at any time, but Penny had assured him she would take care of it, and began working a complicated bit of dragon magic. By the time Mila had come out of her room, her black tights and puffy vest replaced by jeans and a hooded gray long-sleeved shirt, Penny had finished her draconic spell.

It was pretty simple, and Finn was ashamed he hadn't thought of it first. Basically, she'd laced the entire top floor of the building with an out of mind spell. Usually, a spell like that would target everyone who wasn't the caster, making the object slide out of the viewer's mind as soon as they saw it. What made Penny's version so good was she targeted anyone of gnome descent, which the Kashgar were. To everyone else, the place would look normal, but gnomes would think it was just a three-story building.

During the walk to the train and the subsequent long ride to the airport, Mila had been quiet. Finn was worried she was mad at him for some reason he couldn't fathom, a habit he found most of the women in his father's court doing all the time, but a talon in his back from where Penny rode in her hammock on his harness let him know he should say something.

They were walking toward the counters at the airport where they would buy their tickets to Ontario when he finally spoke up.

"Are you doing okay?"

Mila stopped and turned to him, grimacing. "Yeah, I'm fine. That's what bothers me. I saw a guy get stabbed right in front of me, and I'm fine. I think there might be something wrong with me."

Finn laughed, relief flooding through him. "Oh, I was afraid you were mad at me. I didn't know that was the first stabbing you had ever seen."

One of Mila's eyebrows rose slowly as she regarded him. "When would I have ever seen someone stabbed to death?"

Finn shrugged. "I don't know. Things happen. Haven't you ever had to fight someone for an artifact?"

"No. That's not how things are done here on Earth."

They arrived at the counter, and Finn was glad to see there was no one in line.

A young woman at the computer terminal smiled at them. "How may I help you today?"

Mila was still shaking her head at Finn's comment, but

she quickly jumped in, to his great relief. He was still having trouble talking to Nonmagicals.

"We would like two tickets to Toronto, please. first class." She jerked a thumb at Finn, "He's paying. We will be returning in the morning. The earlier, the better."

The woman laughed politely as she clacked away on her keys. After a few minutes, she nodded. "Okay, I have a flight leaving in thirty minutes. The return flight leaves Toronto at five AM. Do you both have your passports?"

Mila handed hers over the counter, having to stand on her tiptoes to do so, while Finn handed over a piece of printer paper that had been folded into fourths. The look on Mila's face almost made Finn laugh out loud, but he contained himself for the sake of the transaction.

Mila opened her mouth to say something but stopped when she saw the woman looking over the folded paper as if nothing was out of the ordinary. She entered the information she saw and handed back both of their passports.

"Two first-class tickets. That will be $3,748. How will you be paying today?" she asked politely, as Mila looked from the paper to the attendant and back again, her eyebrows threatening to crawl off her face from shock.

"Cash, I think." Finn pulled out a stack of hundreds and began counting.

"Oh, that's unusual," the attendant said, glancing from the cash to the large, bearded man counting it out.

"Is it?" He smiled and handed her thirty-eight hundreds. "It's a work thing, so they sent us with what was in the office."

The attendant shrugged and printed their tickets.

155

"You'll be leaving from gate B22. You should probably hurry since they will be boarding in just a few minutes."

Finn took the tickets and gave her a warm smile. "Thank you so much."

Security was even less of a problem, to Mila's amazement. Finn showed the same folded piece of paper and was waved through without a second glance. The scanner concerned Finn, not knowing if Penny would be able to hide from the tech, so he opted for a pat-down instead. He almost laughed when Penny had to scramble around in his jacket—her talons tickled something fierce—but he was cleared without a problem.

They had to run to the gate and made it with only five minutes to spare. Twenty minutes after that, they were in the air, sipping cocktails.

"Okay, how did that work?" Mila asked after taking a sip of her G&T.

"How did what work?" Finn was genuinely confused.

She huffed and threw a hand up. "The paper thing. Passports are notoriously hard to fake, and you just gave her a blank sheet of paper."

Finn chuckled and pulled out the "passport," handing it to her.

"It's not blank," he told her.

She opened the paper and saw that there were small purple runes etched on the corner. They glowed slightly, and she could smell a hint of pine coming from them.

"I don't understand. I mean, I get that it's magic, but it still looks like a piece of paper to me."

"That's because there is something special about you. You haven't woken up, like the Peabrains at the market, but you know there's more to the world than you understand. This is a very simple spell that makes the viewer see what they think they should be seeing. If they expect a passport, then it looks exactly like it should to them. It only works on people who are either nonmagical or not paying very close attention. Usually, it's pretty worthless, but I can see us getting some real mileage out of it here on *Earth*."

"You're telling me you have a literal pass to everything?" Mila asked, the gears in her head turning so hard, Finn would have sworn there was smoke.

"Well, it won't fool electronics, but pretty much, yeah." He settled back in the large chair and sighed.

"Chi chi." Penny poked him in the side, where she was wedged out of sight between him and the armrest.

Finn handed her his package of cookies, then closed his eyes. He was beat, and he fully planned on using the four-hour flight to catch up on some sorely missed sleep. Mila must have had the same thought because he didn't hear another peep from her.

Four hours later, the plane landed and jarred him awake with a start.

Finn saw that the entertainment screen was playing a movie that he hadn't turned on, and when he glanced down to his side, he saw Penny sitting on her haunches, watching with rapt attention, the complimentary headphones held up to her tiny head.

Finn chuckled. "Good flight, was it?"

Penny shrugged, kicking several empty cookie bags onto the floor. She never took her eyes off the screen, enthralled by the ending of *Deadpool 2*.

If Finn knew anything about Penny, she would have made it a mini-marathon, and started with the first one.

"Where did you get... You know what, I don't even want to know."

He turned and saw Mila had slept through the landing. Her head was lolled to the side, facing him. Her lips were parted slightly, with a bead of drool glistening in the corner of her mouth.

He smiled, taking in her peaceful expression. She was a person who liked to know what was happening and figured out how to solve the problem. In the short time he had known her, she had been willing to stretch her understanding of her world to the maximum, but only after she was given evidence, like the market and seeing Fragar for herself. Seeing her at peace, the weight of the world not pressing down on her, made him want to let her continue resting, but the plane was pulling up to the gate, and the stewardess was making the rounds.

He reached out and lightly shook her shoulder. "Mila. We're here," he said gently.

Her eyes fluttered open, and she smacked her lips a few times, wiping the drool from her cheek with an embarrassed smile. "God, I needed that. I hadn't realized just how tired I was."

"Me too. Since landing on *Earth*, the only sleep I've had was the few hours on your couch."

Mila looked past him at Penny, who was putting the headphones back in the bag now that the credits were rolling on her movie.

"Doesn't Penny ever sleep? She didn't even take a nap last night," she pointed out.

Finn glanced down at the little blue dragon. "She only needs to sleep every few days, and even then, only for a few hours. Dragons run on magic more than calories, though she does use calories to make magic, which is why she is always eating."

He had a thought and checked his jacket pocket. The box of Charleston Chew Minis was empty.

"It's also why she will steal the food from your pocket when you're not looking."

Penny had the good grace to look bashful, but she didn't apologize. They had been together for far too long for Finn to expect anything different from her.

He chuckled at her. "It's fine, we'll pick some more up on the way out of the airport."

That made Penny's eyes sparkle before she slipped into his jacket and worked her way back into her hammock at the small of his back.

Mila rented them a car, since they needed a credit card on file, and was bitterly disappointed they didn't have any Challengers available. They ended up in a subcompact that made Finn do some serious folding to get into and out of. When the attendant asked if she wanted to purchase insurance, she started to say no, but then looked at Finn, and furrowed her brow before saying she would take the coverage. Finn wasn't sure if that was a dig at him or not but decided it was better to let it go if it was.

Half an hour and one stop for Charleston Chews later, they pulled into the employee parking lot at the Royal Ontario Museum. The sun was well past set, and the museum had closed for the day, but a very old man stood at the back door. He held it open with a foot and waved to them when they got out of the tiny car.

Mila waved back as she started toward the slightly stooped old man. "Hello, Gregory. Thank you so much for helping us out."

"It's no problem for my favorite student. Who's your large friend there?" he asked, his voice strong despite his age.

"This is Finn. Finn, this is Dr. Gregory Hoffensteffer. He was my professor in graduate school. He's the one who got me fascinated in history," Mila said by way of introduction, an affectionate smile on her face.

Finn held out a hand and was surprised by how firm Gregory's grip was. It seemed the old guy was sprier than he looked. "It's a pleasure to meet you, Doctor Hoffensteffer."

"Please, call me Gregory. I'm too old to wait for you to get that out every time." He waved them inside. "Come on in. It's a little too chilly outside for these old bones."

Finn like the old man instantly. No fuss, no mess, just get on with it. He was just the kind of person Finn liked to work with.

Gregory moved at a pretty good clip, considering he looked to be in his eighties. They passed through some storage rooms, dark now that the place was shut down for the night, but Gregory never missed a step.

Eventually, they came to an office that was very similar to Mila's, except that it was bigger and messier. Wooden crates lined one wall, the tops removed and leaning against their sides. Each one was filled with straw packing material, and several bagged items were poking out. Most of the items were rusted or in some other form of disrepair, except for three which had been moved to the center table and removed from their labeled bags.

Finn moved to the center table and smiled when he saw the Helm of Awe front and center.

It was a steel bucket helmet with very little ornamentation, aside from some scrollwork carved into the mirror-like surface. It looked as though it were brand new, untouched by tarnish. Finn leaned in and inspected the scrollwork. Sure enough, there was Fafnir's signature nestled into the spells written across the helmet's surface.

"I'm really sorry to have to ask you this, Gregory, but can you tell me where the nearest bathroom is? I haven't gone since Denver, and I think I might pee myself after having the coffee I picked up on the way out of the airport." Finn turned to see Mila nearly dancing with her need to relieve herself.

Gregory chuckled. "Just out in the hall and to the left. Then the second right, and that will take you to the lobby. The office bathroom is in the middle of a remodel, so we have to hoof it all the way out there. Here, take my key card to get back through the security doors on your way back."

She grabbed the offered card and nearly ran from the room, waving the card over her shoulder. "Thanks! I'll be right back."

Gregory and Finn watched her go, then the old man turned to him, and his smile was replaced with a frown. "I can't quite figure it out."

Finn's eyebrow rose slowly. "Figure what out?"

A bony finger shot toward Finn and the old man stood

up straight and tall, not showing any of the previous signs of his age. "You, my boy. What are you? You're not an elf, and I've never seen a gnome that tall, unless you count those damn Kashgar. Which I don't, mind you, but you have a similar smell about you."

Ten talons poked into his back in alarm, and he nearly cried out from the pain. He was going to have to trim those things if she was going to keep stabbing him.

As far as Finn was concerned, the jig was up, to some extent.

He opened one side of his jacket. "Come on out. This fella seems to know a thing or two. No use hiding, especially if you're going to be stabbing me every ten minutes."

Penny's head slowly came around his torso and blinked a few times at Gregory. The old man raised an eyebrow but didn't say anything.

Penny frowned up at Finn and huffed a bit of flame before climbing out and up onto his shoulder. "Squee shiri, chi?"

Finn rolled his eyes and handed her the new box of mini chews. "Gregory, meet Penny. Penny...well, you were there."

She regarded Gregory with a critical eye, nearly as hard as the old man did to her. They seemed to be sizing one another up. Finn was glad this guy knew about the magical world. It would make convincing him to hand over the helm that much easier.

Eventually, Gregory smiled. "Hello, there. Am I to assume you are a faerie dragon, then? I didn't think there were any left on Earth after the great hunts during the Dark Ages."

Both Finn and Penny sucked in breaths at that. "Wait, you hunted the intelligent dragons? Wyverns I can see, but the sentient ones as well?"

Gregory shrugged. "We don't really know what happened back then. That's why we call them the Dark Ages, not because it was bleak and grim. Which, now that I think about it, isn't wrong either, but it's mostly because there are very few records from that period. Religion and all that." He walked over to a counter and turned on an electric kettle. "Tea?"

Finn, still rattled to learn that dragons had been so abused here in the past, sat on one of the many stools around the central table. "That would be nice. Do you have any whiskey to put in it?"

"I think I can scrounge some up," he said over his shoulder, busily dropping tea bags into four mugs.

"Now I'm wondering what exactly *you* are." Finn decided to go on the offensive. "I can tell that you're a Peabrain, but I don't see any magical aura like I normally would with someone attuned to the energies. Are you using a concealment spell of some kind?"

Gregory laughed and started pouring steaming water from the kettle. "No, nothing so special. I'm just really old. Once you live as long as I have, you start to see where the edges of the world are a bit blurry. Maybe you slip in for a peek. You don't have to use magic to be aware of it."

"You don't look that old. I mean, you look old, but not *that* old."

Finn took two of the offered mugs and held them while Gregory poured a finger of whiskey into one. The man

163

glanced up at Penny, who nodded, and he gave her a shot as well.

"I'm just over two hundred years old," he said with a toothy smile.

Finn cocked his head to the side. "But you are a Peabrain, right? How is that possible?"

Gregory held up his right hand. On the middle finger was a gold ring that didn't look all that impressive until Finn stared at it and noticed the telltale magical aura.

"Percival's ring. You know, the knight of the Round Table? It's the ring he took from the sleeping maiden."

Finn had no idea what a round table had to do with anything, but Gregory seemed to think he should, so he just nodded. "What does it do?"

A sigh escaped Gregory's lips. "The legends say it makes the wearer impossible to kill. It's worked so far. But I can't take the damned thing off, and every magical I've come across has no clue how it works. I do get older, but at an incredibly slow rate. Found it back at the turn of the last century on a dig. Slipped it on, and I have been stuck with it since."

"That's handy," Finn said, only looking at the up side.

"Sure, it's nice to know that I'm not going out in some random accident, but to tell you the truth, I would rather not have to start my life over with a new identity every thirty years or so. It's a real pain in the ass. But enough about me. What are you?"

Finn smiled. "I'm a dwarf."

Gregory barked out a laugh. "Aren't you all supposed to be short and stubby and carry an axe or something?"

"Why do people keep thinking dwarves are short?" Finn asked, truly bemused.

"It's what the legends say. How is it I've never seen another dwarf in all my years? I know they once existed, but as far as I can tell, they all died out."

Mila came running into the room, breathing deeply, and slammed the door behind her. "We have a problem. A really big problem."

Finn jumped to his feet, Fragar coming out and unfolding an instant later. "What is it?"

Penny hissed on his shoulder, mirroring his intensity.

"I think a group of those Kashgar assholes just broke into the museum." She started to look for a weapon. "I was crossing the lobby when the front door melted. At least eight guys came running through, but there could have been more. I heard the guy in front say to spread out and find the dwarf."

"Goddamned Kashgar!" Gregory shouted, stepping up to the table beside Finn. "Here, Mila, take this. Finn will be able to tell you how to activate it, I never could figure out that damned complicated language they use." He tossed to her what looked like the gold handle of a sword.

She caught it in midair and blinked a few times in surprise. "Gregory, what the fuck? I feel like I missed a few things while I was off peeing."

"You have no idea, but we can talk about it later," Finn said, stepping close and inspecting the handle. He smiled. "This is Gram! Where did you find it?"

"It was with the helm, but I didn't realize it was *that* sword," Gregory admitted, picking up the helm.

Finn leaned in and whispered a word to Mila. Then he

told her, "Don't say it out loud, only quietly to yourself, like I do with Fragar. And mind the pointy end."

Mila glanced at him but nodded, holding the handle in both hands. He saw her lips move, then she jumped back in shock, nearly dropping the handle as a golden blade unfolded from it. In a split second, she was holding a three-foot-long, golden longsword that glowed faintly purple for a few seconds. The blade was covered in runes, just like Fragar.

Gregory was approaching her with the helm, preparing to put it on her head, to Finn's relief, when the door exploded inward, and Mila and Gregory were thrown across the room.

CHAPTER SEVENTEEN

Penny leaped off Finn's shoulder and sent a blast of white-hot flame into the smoking remains of the door. A scream let them know she had caught one of their attackers off guard, and more than likely melted their face.

Finn wasted no time, charging blindly into the smoke, chopping sideways with Fragar, and feeling the blade sink into flesh, eliciting another scream from a second Kashgar attacker. Finn smiled, feeling his blood beginning to rise. Before he could take a second swing, two bodies came flying past their fallen partner and tackled Finn to the ground.

He grunted as the air was forced from his lungs, but he quickly raised a knee, catching the Kashgar on his right between the legs, and with ball-crushing force, knocked him off his right arm.

Several more men and a few women came pouring into the room, most of whom surrounded Finn and began to cast ensnaring spells. Tendrils of golden light spun out from their fingers, trailing tight chains of bubbles. The room suddenly filled with the smell of wildflowers as magic poured from them.

Finn was still pinned by one determined blond-haired man and was unable to avoid the spells.

Penny, on the other hand, was once again overlooked by their attackers and took the opportunity to wreak havoc on the casters. She swooped down from the ceiling and raked her talons across one woman's shoulder and chest while breathing a tight jet of flame into the back of the man next to her.

The woman and man both screamed and lost their concentration. The man flailed about before dropping to the floor to roll about to extinguish the magical flames. The other two casters changed targets to focus on Penny, thinking she was the more dangerous threat.

They were wrong.

"Colbh cloiche."

The words rang out of Finn with a command the earth couldn't deny. He was a dwarf, and as such, the rocky bits of the universe had a special relationship with him.

The smell of wildflowers was suddenly overpowered by a strong scent of pine as a pillar of granite shot from the ground at an angle, ripping a hole in the carpet, and slamming into the chest of one of the last two casters. He was thrown across the room to slam into the wall, ten feet off the ground, and came crashing down on a table covered in pottery that shattered upon impact.

The last caster hesitated, now unsure who to attack.

Penny took the opportunity to rake four deep gouges into his cheek and neck. Finn tossed Fragar with his fee arm, burying the blade in the Kashgar's chest, and dropping him to the ground.

Turning, Finn looked the blond man hanging on his left arm in the eye. The other man's eyes widened when he realized the attack had gone terribly for his people.

"Look, man. This will all go a whole lot better for you if you just give up. We can find you wherever you go," he sputtered out.

Finn punched him in the face with his right hand, knocking the man unconscious in a single blow. A figure raced past him and out the door.

"No!" Mila shouted, pointing at the fleeing woman. "She has the helm. Stop her!"

Penny flapped her large wings, diving through the door. As soon as she was through, there was another explosion that knocked her back into the room to tumble across the floor. She rolled to her feet but stumbled to the side, stunned, and had to sit and shake her head to clear it.

Mila stood over a Kashgar who had attacked her in concert with the one that got away. Gram dripped blood, and the man was missing a hand. He mumbled a spell, covering the stump with a cascade of bubbles that staunched the bleeding before he passed out.

As soon as the attack was over, large bubbles appeared over each of the Kashgar's heads, then popped, erasing their memories. This time, however, there was a bit of red ooze clinging to a few of their faces, and a smell like rotting wood wafted on the breeze.

Gregory shakily climbed to his feet, using an overturned table for support. "Shit, those fellas came out of nowhere. I'm assuming you need that helm, and that they're not going to hand it over easily."

"Yeah," Mila said with a frown. "I'm really sorry about all this."

"It's fine." He waved her concern away. "I understand you didn't feel like you could just come out and say you knew about the other world here on Earth. After all, I didn't tell you I was aware of it either. This is a delicate game we're playing." He put his hands on his hips and looked around at all the dead or unconscious bodies. "You two need to get out of here before I call the authorities. This isn't the first time I've had to clean up something like this."

"Wait, what?" Mila was lost.

Finn saw a small swatch of silver chainmail on the ground and picked it up to inspect it. "I can fill her in on the plane ride home. You're sure you don't need any help here?"

"I have some friends I can call. I'll leave one or two and tell the cops it was a robbery gone bad," Gregory confirmed. "If you get caught up in this, they won't let you back into the U.S. until it is all cleared up, and I have a feeling you're working against a deadline."

Finn nodded and held up the chainmail. "Do you mind if I take this with us?"

"I'll just add it to the things they stole. I'll call it something else, though, so no one catches you with it." He winked and waved them toward the door. "It was a pleasure meeting you, Finn and Penny. I'm sure we can talk more later when there isn't such a large mess to clean up. Mila, you should hang on to this one. He's special."

"Thank you, Gregory. I won't forget this," Finn said, shaking the elderly man's hand.

Gregory smiled. "A favor from a dwarf king. I can live with that."

While Finn hadn't exactly agreed to a favor, he was willing to give one to Mila's old teacher. Not to mention, getting his hands on Gram and the chainmail was worth a favor. "I look forward to hearing what I can do for you."

Finn took Mila's hand and led her into the hall. She was looking over her shoulder at Gregory, who gave her a friendly wave. "Talk to you later, dear. Remember, stick close to that one."

Penny shot Gregory a smile and a wave before flying after them.

The car ride back to the airport and the process of buying tickets and getting through security passed in relative silence. Mila kept almost talking, only to clam up at the last second. Finn was glad for her silence since it let him think through the problem of how the Kashgar kept finding them.

At the apartment, he'd thought they had just followed him from the market, but to be attacked in another country altogether meant they were either keeping very close watch of him or they had a way of finding him through magical means. But if they were finding him through magical means, then they had to have put a tracking spell on him at some point, and he would have smelled the magic.

Then it hit him. When he had mentioned the Dark Star to the Huldu in the market, the elf he had bought the healing potions off of had begun to act strange, as if she knew exactly who he was talking about. Plus, the entire market had reeked of magic at every turn.

Finn suddenly became very suspicious that he knew exactly what had happened.

Scanning for somewhere private, he spotted a family restroom and took Mila's hand, pulling her toward the door.

"Hey, whoa," she protested as she was pulled off balance. "Where are we going?"

"Sorry." He gave her a reassuring smile. "I just realized how those Kashgar keep finding us. I need your help."

"Okay, all you need to do is ask. Quit just pulling me around," she retorted, a little heat in her voice.

Finn let go of her hand, realization dawning that he was not trusting her like he should.

"Sorry. I'm not very used to people wanting to help. Out there, life is a little lonely for a dwarf. Most people don't like us, due to my kind ruling over them."

"Okay, I understand that, but you need to remember that all that baggage you picked up *out there* doesn't mean shit *here*. I don't have a problem with you because you're a dwarf. My problem is that you keep dragging me around by the hand. I can make my own decisions, and I can see that the world is a whole lot bigger than I thought it was just a day ago. It's taken me a while to grasp just how big, but I already told you I'm in. Just talk to me."

Finn took a deep breath. He'd never met anyone quite like Mila. She was strong and determined, and for whatever reason, she kept sticking her neck out for him. The least he could do was trust her judgment. After all, she was the expert when it came to *Earth* and their social interactions. And she had shown herself to be a friend. The least he could do was offer the same for her.

"You're right. I am sorry." He gave her a slight bow with his head. "I will learn to trust your judgment. And stop pulling you around by the hand. Unless you're in danger— then I'm pulling with everything I've got."

"Okay, that's more like it," she said gently. "Now, what's this revelation you had that entails dragging me to a bathroom?" She knocked on the family bathroom door for emphasis.

"I think that elf in the market put a tracking spell on me. I need you to find it so Penny can remove it."

She raised an eyebrow. "Can't Penny find it?"

Finn gave her a chagrined smile. "Unfortunately, she can't. Faerie dragons see with magical sight. Mundane things look normal to her, but magical things glow. When she looks at magical creatures, there is a light coming off of them that will mask any spells on their bodies. It would be like us trying to spot something on our bodies the same temperature as our skin through thermal goggles. You guys have those, right? Thermal goggles?"

"Yeah, we have those. But there's a problem with your plan." She gave him a look as if he should be able to guess. After a few beats, it was obvious to her that he was at a loss. She rolled her eyes. "I can't see magic at all. How am I supposed to spot a spell on you?"

He made an O face, then shrugged. "You can see magic, though. You saw the runes on my head when we first met."

"Yeah, but I can't see them now," she protested.

He sighed. "We have to try. What's the point if they know where we are all the time? Eventually, they'll track us when we're at the ship, then this whole thing is for naught. Besides, we will never find your friend Jeff if they know we're coming."

She pursed her lips, then nodded. "Okay, we can give it a shot. But if it doesn't work, we'll have to wait until we get home and Danica can take a look at you."

Finn rolled his eyes. "Good fucking point. Let's just do that. Danica can help you spot the mark so that next time you can do it on your own."

Mila laughed. "See, asking me is already paying off. Come on, let's get on the plane. There's a mimosa waiting with my name on it."

"What's a mimosa?" Finn asked, following her toward their gate.

She took his hand this time and smiled up at him. "Oh, buddy. You haven't lived until you've had one. Come on. It seems I have a lot to teach you about this strange and wonderful world you two landed on."

CHAPTER EIGHTEEN

The flight back gave Finn a chance to indulge in the first-class wares. To the flight attendant's shock, and Mila's chagrin, he ended up having roughly fifteen mimosas, which wasn't even close to enough to get him drunk but did give him a mild buzz.

After scanning the movie selection, he decided on one that he had seen before—*The Alamo* starring John Wayne, his favorite actor. Of all the movies he had recorded on the *Anthem*, the John Wayne movies held a special place in his heart. The guy's cocksure manner and ability to say the right thing at the right time made Finn realize just how badass a Peabrain could be, and the guy never once used magic, which blew Finn's mind.

Now that they were on *Earth*, the fact that the Duke didn't use magic made a whole lot more sense.

Mila took the chance to sleep and was out for most of the trip, snoring softly, and occasionally rolling over in the reclined chair. Finn asked for a blanket and covered her when he saw her shivering in the air conditioning.

Penny, having seen *The Alamo* several times and not sharing Finn's obsession with John Wayne, crawled from his seat to Mila's and curled up under the blanket with her.

They landed at 8:00 AM local time and jumped on the train after a long walk through Denver International. By nine, Mila was slipping her key into the front door of her condo and running to the bathroom.

Finn figured out the coffee pot and made the strongest coffee he could, while Mila changed into something more comfortable—a pair of tights and a baggy t-shirt.

They sat on the balcony overlooking Coors Field and the mountains in the distance behind it. Mila slouched in her chair, her bare feet on the railing, and sipped her mug of steaming black coffee while Finn dropped a few of the Charleston Chews into his and stirred it with a spoon. Penny skipped the coffee and just ate from a small pile of the little chocolate-covered nougats.

Conversation was sparse, each of them enjoying the calm before the storm they knew was coming. Mila said that Danica should be home around noon from her shift at the hospital, and right on cue, the front door opened to reveal the tall blonde elf, looking as fresh as she had the day before when she had left.

"Hey, guys," she shouted through the open balcony doors as she kicked her black heels off beside the front door and dropped her purse on the counter. She poured herself a cup of coffee and padded out to meet them. "You been lazing around all day?"

"Nope. We went to Toronto and got in a fight with, like, ten guys," Finn said, smiling up at her.

"I chopped a guy's hand off," Mila added, making Danica snort coffee out of her nose.

Penny cocked a smile. "Shirirt shi chir chi." She blew a little flame for emphasis.

"She says she melted a guy's face. We're not entirely sure on that one. There was a lot of smoke at the time," Finn translated.

Danica sat in one of the empty chairs. "Holy shit. Did you at least get what you went for?"

Finn sucked in a slow breath. "Well, not exactly. We did get Mila a sword. Oh, that reminds me." He pulled the chainmail from his pocket and handed it to Mila. "This might help if you're going to keep hanging out with me."

Mila took the small metal swatch and inspected it. "What is it?"

"Armor," Finn said as if it were obvious. "Remember the power word for Gram? Well, just add 'Ka' to the beginning of it, and it will activate the armor."

Danica leaned in and inspected the silver mail. "Oh, my God. Is that dwarven mithril?"

"Yeah. It's a pretty basic piece, so it'll only cover your torso, but it's tough stuff. Give it a try."

Mila put down her coffee and stood up, holding the swatch. She said the power word, almost mouthing it, and the links began to glow purple before the entire swatch melted and soaked into her hand. She gave a yelp of surprise and pulled the collar of her shirt forward, looking down it.

"Holy shit. It's on my skin, even under my bra. Is it supposed to do that?"

"Yeah, that stuff is like dragon scales. It conforms to the

wearer's body for maximum movement while making you nearly impenetrable." Finn held up his coffee in a toast. "Congratulations, you're bulletproof."

Mila pulled her shirt over her head, exposing the links that clung to her like a wet t-shirt, showing the lines of her tight abdomen and even the indentation of her belly button.

"The links are so close-knit, you can't even see through them!" she exclaimed.

Before anyone could stop her, she reached back and unclasped her bra, letting it fall forward onto her arms, and exposing her chain-link-covered breasts in perfect detail.

Finn shot coffee out of his nose and turned crimson before looking away. Mila realized just how form-fitting the armor was just a little too late and quickly pulled her bra back up. Danica nearly spilled her coffee down her white blouse, she was laughing so hard.

"You should probably keep your clothes on, sweetie. This is more of an under-armor situation, I think." The elf chuckled, wiping tears from her eyes, and glanced at Finn, which made her laugh even more.

Mila, red-faced but laughing along with Danica, fastened her bra again but didn't put her t-shirt back on. "Where does it go when I take it off?"

She quietly said the activation word again, and the silver rings melted into her skin. She held out her hand, expecting the swatch to reappear, but nothing happened.

"Oh shit!" Danica's eyebrows went up two inches in surprise. "That's a bonded piece. I didn't know there were any of those left."

"A what? Where did it go?" Mila began feeling the skin

of her stomach and hips as if the swatch were stuck to her somewhere.

"It's part of you now," Danica explained. "There's a power word to remove it, but if you don't say it, the armor is with you until you die. It's incredibly powerful and expensive. I can't even begin to guess what that is worth."

Mila said the power word again and the armor formed on her in the blink of an eye. She said it a fourth time and it disappeared.

"It's not going to, like, give me cancer or something, is it?" Once again, she activated the armor, this time leaving it exposed.

"No, it's perfectly safe," Danica reassured her. "In fact, people who have an active magical artifact have a much lower chance of being sick. We think it's a byproduct of having magic constantly flowing through you. If anything, your life span just increased."

Mila pulled the waistband of her tights open to see how far down the armor went, and her eyes widened. She pulled the back of the tights away and twisted to get a view of her behind. "This thing goes all the way around like a bathing suit. I thought you said it only protected the torso?"

Finn cleared his throat, doing his best not to look at her as she inspected herself. "Well, some would argue that the crotch is the most important part of the torso. You would be surprised how often it gets hit during a fight."

Mila chuckled and gave him a sly smile. "Know that from experience, do you?"

"Well, yes," he admitted. "Usually, though, I'm doing the

hitting. It's like an off-switch to a fight. One good hit and they are not coming after you for a good long while."

Penny chuckled at some memory, popped a mini into her mouth, and reclined on the table. "Squee shi grii." She laughed at the look of betrayal on Finn's face at her words.

"What?" Mila asked, a smile creeping across her lips.

Finn sighed. "She was reminding me of the last time that particular move was used on me. I may have thrown up."

Mila laughed, then jumped when Danica touched a spot on her back. "Whoa, your fingers are cold."

"Take the armor off again," Danica said in her doctor's voice.

Mila said the power word and the armor melted away, leaving her back exposed. Danica leaned in and blew on the spot. A small trail of bubbles shot out and popped on Mila's skin, accompanied by a lavender smell.

"What's this?" she asked Finn, grabbing Mila's hips and turning her toward him. "Did you put this on her?"

Finn saw a set of marks that glowed faintly pink, now that Danica had used a little magic to brighten them. The spot was about the size of a fingerprint, located just above her right kidney.

"Oh, shit," Finn groaned. "They weren't tracking me. They were tracking you, Mila. It must have been that elf in the market. She probably touched you and transferred the mark as she walked past. No wonder I didn't feel anything."

Penny was up on his shoulder in an instant, leaning in to get a closer look. Her eyes flicked down and she pointed a talon at something poking over the hem of Mila's tights at her lower back. "Chi gri?" she asked.

Finn looked to where Penny was pointing, and saw the top of a tattoo. It looked like the top of a blond person with spiky hair, and the top half of a cartoon tiger.

"Is that another spell?" he asked, poking a finger into the waistband of her tights and starting to pull it down.

Mila quickly grabbed his hand and pulled the waistband up until the tattoo was hidden completely. "No, that's a really bad choice I made back in undergrad. No need to show that off."

Finn was interested, but she obviously didn't want to show him what it was. He focused on the tracking spell and looked at Penny. "Can you take care of it?"

Penny cocked her head and shrugged. "Chi chi."

Finn rolled his eyes. "I know you can't see it, but you can feel it, can't you?"

Penny considered that while pressing a hand to the mark. She concentrated, then shook her head. "Shiri geri."

"Shit." Finn looked at Danica. "I'm crap when it comes to the fine kinds of magic. Can you do anything about it?"

Danica nodded. "I can remove it, but I'll need to get some components. Wait here, I'll be right back." She set her cup on the table and went to her room.

"A bad choice in undergrad, eh?" he teased.

Mila huffed and turned to face him, one of her eyebrows rising. "I don't want to talk about it. Give me one of those chews."

He laughed, fished a few of the chocolates from the box on the table, and handed them to her. She bit one in half and chewed slowly, looking out over the city.

"Why did you give me the armor? Danica said it was expensive. Aren't you a treasure hunter for profit? You could have sold it." She crossed her arms and looked at the mountains, avoiding eye contact.

Finn leaned back and retrieved his mug of coffee, taking a long pull before answering. "Because a trusted ally is worth all the Thul in the universe. Think of it as an investment. And it'll go great with Gram."

"You're giving me the sword too?" she asked, turning to him with one eyebrow raised.

He shrugged. "You seem to know your way around it well enough, although I should probably start teaching you how to properly use it. Besides, I have Fragar. He suits me better."

She turned and leaned her hip on the rail, her arms still crossed. "So, you expect me to keep on helping you for the long haul?"

"Not at all," he clarified. "Even if you don't want anything to do with me after this is all over, the armor and Gram are yours to do with as you like. They're a gift. No strings attached."

Penny was watching the two of them as if they were playing a rather interesting game of tennis, swiveling her head back and forth as each one talked.

"Okay, I can accept a gift." She smiled. "It's not like you need the money anyway. There's a safe in there with a year's salary, plus four more golden nuggets worth the same. What exactly is your plan here, anyway?"

Finn sucked in a deep breath, giving himself a second to think about that. "Well, first of all, I need to get my ship working so I can help you find your friend. Then I want to look into this Dark Star character. Back at Gregory's office, I noticed there was a little red ooze leftover when the Kashgar's minds were wiped."

"What does that mean?" She frowned with sudden concern.

Finn frowned right along with her. "It means there's some dark magic at play. And that could spell disaster for a lot of people. From the sound of it, this Dark Star has some huge plans, possibly world-changing plans. The wars they could wage would spell disaster for a large portion of the Peabrains that haven't woken up yet."

Danica came out with a small, black leather satchel in her hands. "Did I miss something? The party seems to have soured a bit." She waved for Mila to come over while she sat back down.

Mila pushed off the rail with her hip and turned her back to Danica so she could see the mark. "We were just talking about this Dark Star character. Have you heard anything about her?"

Danica paused, a vial of viscous blue liquid tilted so she could dab a little on her finger. "The Dark Star? Yeah, pretty sure everyone's heard of her. At least heard rumors. Supposedly, the Dark Star is trying to fight for Magicals' rights or some such shit. There's always talk of some group trying to come out into the open, but that's all they end up being; talk."

She touched the blue-covered finger to Mila's back, making the woman suck in a breath.

"Oh, fuck. That's really cold. What the hell is that?"

"Sorry, I should have warned you. It's frost-elemental blood."

Mila looked over her shoulder with wide eyes. "You're

rubbing blood into my back? Isn't that dangerous from a medical point of view?"

Danica laughed. "Not really. Elementals aren't the same species. Hell, they're not even from the same dimension. There's nothing bloodborne they can give you. It's perfectly safe."

She began to chant, drawing symbols in the air just above the mark on Mila's back with her blue-stained finger.

Finn frowned, only half-watching Danica do her magic. He was more concerned with what she had said about the Dark Star. If there were rumors already flying, then that meant people were putting credence to what was being said, or they wouldn't keep saying it. That meant there could be a lot of supporters behind the scenes.

Maybe this woman was further along with her plans than Finn had originally thought.

A flash of blue light and the sound of popping bubbles heralded the pleasant smell of lavender.

"Done," Danica proclaimed, wiping the residual blue substance from Mila's back with a small towel she had brought with her. "No one will be tracking your cute butt anytime soon." She playfully smacked Mila's ass, making the smaller woman yelp.

"What now?" Mila asked, rubbing her butt cheek with the palm of her hand as Danica packed up her bag.

Finn looked up into her large brown eyes and smiled. "Now we wait. We have something they want, and they have no way of finding us anymore. I'm betting we get a call by this afternoon."

"But they don't have my number." Mila pulled her t-shirt on and sat back down in her chair, propping her bare feet back up on the railing.

Finn closed his eyes, soaking in the sun. "That won't stop them. Let's just enjoy the day until all hell breaks loose."

"If we're just lounging around, then I'm going to change into my lounging pants," Danica declared, standing and walking back inside. "Who wants a beer? I need a beer."

Mila and Finn said, "I do" at the same time.

Penny was only a heartbeat behind with a "Chi!" and a smoke ring from her nostril before biting into her last Charleston Chew.

CHAPTER NINETEEN

Mila reclined into the corner of the large, gray, L-shaped sofa, Danica laying across the short side, her head in Mila's lap as they watched *True Grit*. Not the new one, but the old one with John Wayne. Finn had convinced them to turn it on when Danica had told him they could stream anything he wanted on the TV. Mila had never seen it, but she was enjoying it so far. She had propped her feet on Finn's lap. He was sitting next to her, and practically mouthing the words along with the Duke, completely lost in the movie.

Mila smiled at the big, bearded man and his completely genuine engrossment in the movie. He was such an odd character, even before she factored in that he was actually a dwarf. Halfway through the movie, he had started rubbing the soles of her feet with a thumb. It was absentminded, and in no way did she feel like he was coming on to her. He just did it because it was a nice thing for her. She wasn't even sure he knew he was doing it; it seemed more like his subconscious just made him do thoughtful things without his knowledge.

She had noticed he did that a lot. Unconscious favors or niceties, like helping Penny get a better purchase on his shoulder, or moving to put himself in the more dangerous position, like walking on the street-side of the sidewalk, or holding doors for strangers. The small things that most people didn't even notice, but that added up over time. Not like some men she had met, who would do nice things expecting something in return, or to build up "points," like they were playing some game where trading the most valuable favors was the objective.

She caught Penny staring at her from Finn's shoulder and turned a little red from the scrutiny, not that she had anything to be embarrassed about. When Penny saw her glance, smiled, and puffed a little smoke ring from her nostril. Mila smiled back, understanding that meant Penny approved.

Hopping off Finn's shoulder and onto the back of the couch, Penny came around to rest her head on Mila's shoulder while lying down on the pillow behind her head. She hummed with satisfaction and closed her eyes, resting.

Mila didn't quite know what to make of that. Penny was by all rights just as sentient as the rest of them, maybe even more so, from what Finn had told her, but sometimes, the small dragon acted like a pet. It was a weird combination of mannerisms that confused Mila a bit. In the end, she decided it was best practice to just treat Penny like anyone else she would talk to. She was like a very affectionate person, but she was still a person.

Looking down, she saw Danica gazing at her with her blue eyes twinkling and a smile plastered on her face.

"What?" Mila whispered, not wanting to interrupt the movie for Finn.

Danica just shook her head, but kept the knowing smile on her face, and turned back to the screen. She reached up and patted Mila's leg in a pandering sort of way, but one full of affection at the same time.

"I need to hit the head and grab another beer. You three okay? Want anything?" Finn asked, gently moving Mila's thoroughly massaged feet to the couch and getting up.

"I'm all good." Mila smiled at him.

"I'm good too, thanks," Danica said.

Penny just flicked her tail but he seemed to know exactly what that meant.

Mila watched as he bent over and picked up the four empty bottles of their previous round, and headed into the kitchen to drop them in the recycling before going into the bathroom and closing the door.

She liked that. She didn't think he was a very tidy person naturally, from the small things she'd observed, like how he had just dropped his clothes beside the couch when he went to sleep the other night. That meant he was being tidy for her sake. Just another of the little niceties adding up in her mind.

As soon as the bathroom door closed, Danica was on her knees, looming over Mila, her face about to split in half with a smile. "Okay, what the hell is going on with you two?"

"Chi chi!" Penny agreed, her eyes now wide open and staring at Mila, her own teeth showing in a huge smile.

"Oh my god." Mila sank deeper into the couch to get away from them, but it just trapped her all the more between their creepy smiling faces. "What are you talking about?"

"Oh, don't give me that, Mi. I've known you for ten years, and have only seen you look at a guy that way once. And he was holding a priceless Mayan artifact at the time." Danica leaned in even closer. "You are so into Finn."

Penny leaned in too, nodding and puffing a smoke ring in agreement.

"You would be okay with that?" she asked Penny. Then, when she realized what she was saying, quickly added, "I mean, theoretically."

"Chi. Shirich." Penny emphasized the words just right so that the tone was undeniable. *'Fuck yeah, I'm good with that.'*

Mila barked a nervous laugh. "Guys, come on. I've only known him for two days. You can't fall for someone in two days."

Danica and Penny locked gazes, grinning the whole time. "Who said anything about falling for him? I just wanted to know why I was going to have to start cutting the air with a knife just to get through all this sexual tension." Danica laughed, and Penny puffed flames, chortling right along with her.

Mila rolled her eyes. "Okay, enough. He'll be out any second and see you two acting the fools. Then we'll have to explain why, and that could blow everything. Please just back off. I don't have any comment at this time."

Danica and Penny exchanged another look and nodded before settling back into their respective places as if nothing had happened at all. As soon as Danica's head hit her lap, the bathroom door opened, and Finn walked out, adjusting his belt. He went to the fridge and grabbed a beer, opening it with pure brute strength instead of a bottle opener, and tossed the cap in the garbage before returning to his place on the couch beside her.

"What did I miss?" he asked, seeing the strange look on Mila's face.

Mila felt her cheeks redden. "Nothing," she practically squeaked out, which made both Danica and Penny start laughing.

Finn raised an eyebrow in confusion, but settled back into the couch and took a swig of beer. "Okay. Keep your secrets. I have the Duke."

It took nearly ten minutes before Mila built up the courage to put her feet back on his lap. As soon as she did, he automatically started rubbing one of them with his free hand while he took another sip of his beer.

Danica rolled her head forward and gave Mila a kiss on the thigh before patting her leg affectionately in recognition of her bravery. A warm feeling rose up in Mila's chest, and she started running her fingers through Danica's long, blonde hair with gentle strokes as Pepper told the Duke, *"That's some bold talk for a one-eyed fat man."*

John Wayne charged, guns blazing, and Mila closed her eyes, enjoying the large hand gently rubbing away the soreness of a long couple of days.

Mila woke with a start. She was still on the couch, with

Danica and Penny sleeping on her, but Finn was on his feet pacing, her phone ringing in his hand. He glanced at her and she gave him a nod, understanding right away.

He answered and put the phone to his ear. "About time you called."

She shook Danica awake, who sat up right away, rubbing the sleep from her eyes. Penny didn't need to be awakened, having sat up when Finn spoke. Mila climbed off the couch and waved for him to show her the phone. He did, and she pressed the speakerphone button.

"..for the helm," the voice on the line said.

She recognized the speaker as the man who had attacked them in the park. Luther, or something like it.

"Sorry, Lithor. I didn't get that last part. Care to repeat it?"

Finn smiled at the sigh of frustration on the other end.

"I said, my mistress has told me that she is willing to trade your ship for the Helm of Awe," he repeated, irritation thick in his voice.

"That doesn't seem like a fair trade, now does it?" Finn raised an eyebrow at Mila.

"She thought you might feel that way, so there is a second part to the offer. If you don't trade, she will be forced to destroy the artifact in the middle of downtown," Lithor snarled.

Finn frowned and glanced at Danica, who just shrugged. "Again, I don't really see the problem. I can always find another artifact to suit my needs."

"Did I mention that she will be using a magical feedback loop to destroy the helm? One powered by dark magic, which my mistress is a master of? I'm sure you have heard the rumors, or maybe even seen the aftereffects by now. You know she can and will do it. Just tell me where the ship is, and this will all be over." Lithor's tone had gone from irritated to condescending.

Finn's eyes widened with fear, which scared Mila more than the attacks from the Kashgar had.

"Okay, you have a deal," Finn said. "Can I send text on this thing?"

It took Mila a second to realize that the second part was directed at her, and she nodded quickly.

"I'll send you coordinates where we can meet and make the trade. Give me an hour." Finn ground his teeth in anger, but he was going along with the demands, to Mila's confusion.

"Good, I'm so glad you deci—"

Finn hung up and almost threw the phone before gently putting it on the coffee table and closing his eyes, taking several deep breaths.

Mila licked her lips and cleared her throat. "Um, am I missing something?" She glanced at Danica, who was paler than usual, the front of her t-shirt crumpled in one of her fists. "I'm missing something. Why did you agree to give them your ship? Like you said, we can just find another artifact to trade to the Huldu."

Finn opened his eyes, his calm demeanor back in place. "It's the way they were going to destroy it that matters. This Dark Star is using dark magic. Not many can, and even fewer can survive using it for very long, but it is powerful enough to fracture something like the Helm of Awe."

"Oh, my God," Danica squeaked, a hand flying to her mouth. "That would be…catastrophic on so many levels."

"Why?" Mila hated playing catch-up, but this was a whole new realm of thinking for her. There were just too many variables.

"Using a dark magic feedback loop on an artifact that powerful wouldn't just break the artifact, it would release all its stored magic as well. It would explode," Finn told her as he paced.

"How big an explosion are we talking?"

"Chiri sharoopt," Penny said, her hands mimicking an explosion that kept getting bigger until she couldn't reach any further apart.

"So, big?" Mila guessed.

"Think nuclear-bomb big," Danica confirmed. "It would wipe Denver off the map."

"Oh, my God. That would start a war. Fuck, that would start a world war." Mila's stomach flipped.

"It's not all bad, though." Finn nodded, his smile beginning to peek through his dark beard. "I do have the tracking spell on the *Anthem*. Even if they take it, we can still find her. Probably."

"Can't they just take the spell off, like Danica did to me?" Mila asked.

"No. I use dwarven magic, something unique to my species. Not many others can use it, let alone comprehend it. I think it'll be fine. We just need to trust the universe. It hasn't let me down so far."

"Do you want me to come along?" Danica asked, the worry on her face making it clear that she didn't want anything to do with what was about to go down, but she would go if they needed her.

Finn smiled at her and reached over to squeeze her shoulder. "No. You stay here. I don't want you getting any more mixed up in this than you have to. Although we could use your car again if you don't mind."

Relief played across her face, and she smiled her brilliant smile. "Of course you can. Try not to get it blown up or anything."

"No promises, but I'll buy you a new one if we do," Finn reassured her.

"Well, in that case, you can blow the thing into the stratosphere. I was thinking of updating anyway," she joked, then sobered. "Be careful, you three."

She suddenly reached out and engulfed Mila in a tight hug. Mila hugged her back, but Danica held on tight and whispered in her ear.

"I know we were teasing you earlier, but seriously. Right there is a generous dwarf. I know that doesn't mean much to you, but trust me when I tell you I would have made a bet that a four-headed unicorn would appear in our living room before I ever met a generous dwarf. Hang on to him."

Mila rolled her eyes and whispered back, "I don't even have him."

"If you say so." Danica released her and gave her a kiss on the cheek. "Be careful."

"Yes, Mom," Mila replied but squeezed her hand reassuringly.

CHAPTER TWENTY

Finn bounced his knee as they sat in the Forester, parked in the turnaround on the fire road, overlooking the valley where the *Anthem* sat shrouded in the cloaking spell. The sun was still an hour from setting, but the sky was already turning a burnt orange, and the deep valleys were cast in purple shadow where the mountains behind them blocked the light.

Nervous energy filled the car, mostly from him, but he saw Mila chewing her fingernails from time to time. She checked her phone for the hundredth time since they'd sent the coordinates to Lithor and huffed in frustration when there was nothing on the screen.

"Hey." Finn leaned forward, catching her eye. "We'll be fine. We make the trade, and that will be that. We fight for the *Anthem* another day. One thing at a time."

She gave him a half-hearted smile. "I know, but what's keeping them from just attacking us and taking the ship and the helm and leaving us dead on the side of a mountain?"

Finn was taken aback by her dour outlook but had to smile at her forward thinking. "Because I'm a dwarf. And as far as I know, I'm the only dwarf on the planet. I don't know who this Dark Star is, but she's smart. She knows there is a whole treasure trove of stuff that will be out of her reach without me. Artifacts that will be lost to time without a dwarf to activate them. Right about now, she's probably working on a plan to win me over to her side. She won't kill us; she needs us."

He had no idea if that were true, but it was what Mila needed to hear. He and Penny were planning on fighting their way out if need be. Mila's new armor would keep her alive as long as he was able to get to her side fast enough, and from the lackluster performance the Kashgar had shown so far, he felt confident they could at least get away with their lives.

Finn was a warrior born and raised. So far, he hadn't seen anyone on the *Earth* who stood a chance against him. That wasn't to say he was getting cocky, just the opposite. With each new encounter, he expected the opposition to throw their best at him. There was always someone bigger, badder, and meaner. He just hadn't met them yet.

From the corner of his eye, Finn caught the rainbow sheen of a large bubble forming beside the car.

"Here they come. Be sure to activate your armor, and keep Gram handy." He looked out the window and saw several more bubbles forming.

Mila pulled the handle of Gram out of her hoodie's front pocket. "Got it right here. But I thought you said they wouldn't attack us?"

"Never hurts to be prepared for everything. Besides, I'm

still getting accustomed to the way you people think on this rock." He gave her a toothy grin and patted her thigh. "Come on, don't want to keep them waiting."

He opened the door and climbed out. Glancing down into the valley, he caught a smudge of blue in the grass beside the ship and hoped Penny would keep her cool if things went south. She had a lot more to lose than he did, and she wasn't as tough as she let on.

Well, that probably wasn't true. Penny was one of the toughest people he had ever met, both mentally and physically, but he still worried about her.

In less than two minutes, nearly thirty bubbles had formed, each nearly seven feet in diameter. As if waiting for the last bubble to form, they all popped at once, depositing the same number of Kashgar on the gravel road. Most of them were dressed in street clothes and holding cases Finn assumed held parts for the *Anthem*. Some, however, were dressed in black fatigues and military-style jackets. Each of them held a baton that Finn guessed was augmented either with magic or electric shockers, from the way they all held them away from their bodies. In the center was Lithor, a black patch over the eye Penny had gouged out.

Finn had to suppress a smile at the sight of the patch. It had probably been a rude awakening for old Lithor when he found out faerie dragon talon wounds couldn't be healed by magical means. It was one of the reasons her kind had been hunted to near-extinction.

Lithor spotted Finn and made his way through the crowd until he was standing face to face with the dwarf.

They stared at one another. Well, Lithor half-stared, but Finn knew what he was trying to do.

"Took your sweet-ass time getting here." Finn sniffed and glanced at the thirty-some people behind the one-eyed man. "You planning on having a party or something?"

Lithor pulled a black felt sack off his belt and opened the drawstring, ignoring Finn's banter. He showed the helm to Finn while keeping hold of the sack. "Here's the helm, now where is the ship?"

"I'm going to have to inspect that, you know." Finn pointed at the sack and gave him an apologetic look.

"Don't try anything funny or we will be forced to kill you." The Kashgar pointedly looked past Finn at Mila. "Both of you."

"Yeah, yeah. This ain't my first rodeo. Though, ironically, I've never been to an actual rodeo."

Finn held out his hand, and Lithor handed him the bag. The dwarf fished out the helm and turned it over a few times. He had been sure it was the real thing as soon as he saw it in the open bag, but he was also sure there was a little extra something along with it.

He held the metal close to his face and began to sniff it, turning it over and over until he'd had a good whiff of the whole thing. He almost bought that there were no extra spells etched onto the metal until he sniffed the inside, where there was the faint but unmistakable scent of wildflowers.

He grinned and lowered the helm. "Whoever does your spellwork should know that dwarves have excellent noses. If they had done the spell a few hours earlier, I might have missed it, but..."

He let the comment hang in the air between him and Lithor.

Eventually, Lithor sighed and waved one of his men forward, motioning for him to remove his spell from the inside of the helm. Finn watched, both to make sure the spell was properly removed and to see exactly what it was.

"Really, Lithor? Another tracking spell? Do I look like I was born yesterday?" Finn stuffed the helm into the sack and drew it closed. He waved a hand over his head and whistled loudly through his teeth, making Lithor cringe at the sudden shrill noise.

One second, the valley was empty, the next, it had a five-hundred-foot-diameter asteroid sitting in it for all to see, as Penny started pulling up the markers of the cloaking spell and stuffing them into a small bag she was carrying.

"You should probably hurry if you don't want the locals coming to investigate. I bet they can see the old girl from the city if they squint," Finn said, a smile on his face.

"Get moving, people! We only have an hour to get that thing hidden again," Lithor yelled, his men jumping into action and running down the slope toward the ship. He turned to face Finn one last time. "Don't think we won't kill you and the girl if you try to come after us. Our deal is done. The Dark Star thanks you for your cooperation." He turned on his heel and started after his people at a much more sedate pace.

"God, that guy's an asshole," Mila said, stepping up next to Finn and watching the retreating figures.

"Yeah." He put an arm around her shoulders and gave her a little shake. "See? Nothing to worry about. Told you it would be fine."

She rolled her eyes but didn't pull away. "You also said to keep Gram in hand and wear my armor."

"We'll call it even, then." He smiled.

Looking out over the valley, he spotted Penny flying their way, the now-full bag heavy in her hands. As soon as she was close enough, she dropped the bag into his outstretched arms and landed on his shoulder, breathing deep from her workout.

"Shi chi?" she asked, shaking her wings out.

"Yup, got it right here." He patted the black felt bag. "Checked it for spells, and sure enough, they had one on the inside. Watched him take it off. We're good to go."

"Gri chi?" She cocked her head to the side.

Finn froze, his mouth open to protest, but instead lifted the bag to his nose and began sniffing. "Fuck me. I guess I *was* born yesterday," he admitted.

He pulled the helm from the sack and held it up in front of Penny. She had the decency to not say she told him so and instead blew a steady flame onto the bottom of the bag, catching it on fire. The flames engulfed the felt almost too quickly for Finn to toss it to the gravel road.

"There was a second spell on the bag, wasn't there?" Mila asked, a knowing smile on her face.

"Yeah. Yeah, there was." He opened the car door and climbed in. "I don't want to talk about it. Let's go before they realize we found the second spell and decide to do something about it."

Mila climbed in and started the car. Backing up, she turned the car around and started down the mountain. "Where to?"

"The market. We need to meet with the Huldu tonight.

We don't need the parts anymore, but we will need their help eventually, and nothing buys a favor like a nice hefty gift."

"Did you learn that from your time in your father's court?" Mila asked, carefully making a turn that blocked Finn's view of the *Anthem*.

"Nope. *The Godfather*," he said, craning his neck when they made another turn and the valley was exposed once again. He could see the *Anthem* covered in bubbles tinged with red.

"Is that some kind of title? Like a wise man or something?"

He could tell she was making conversation to distract him from what had just happened, and he appreciated it, but her not knowing what *The Godfather* was made him recoil.

"No, it's a movie. Have you never seen *The Godfather*?"

"Nope. I heard it was pretty good, though."

She turned again, bringing the ship into view...or at least, the area where the ship had been moments ago. Now there was only the burned-out crater where the *Anthem* had landed three days before.

"Maybe we can watch it together," she suggested, giving him a smile that faded when she saw the ship was gone. "Sorry. I know she meant a lot to you." She squeezed his knee and gave him a sad smile before turning back to the road.

Finn sucked in a breath. "It's fine. I'll start tracking her once we get home. Don't want to warn them too early that we know where they are, just in case they find the spell when I activate it." He calmed his center with a few deep breaths, then turned to Mila and smiled. "I would love to show you *The Godfather*. Maybe when this is all over, we can watch it."

"We can make it a marathon. Watch all of them in a row."

Finn blinked. "There's more than one?"

"Yeah. Three, I think." She laughed at his surprise.

"Then we will definitely have a marathon." He smiled, his spirits lifted.

He looked at Mila, who was concentrating on the road, and caught Penny looking at him from his lap with a stupid grin on her face. She looked from him to Mila and back, the grin still in place, if not a little bigger. All Finn could do was shrug.

She was right, as usual.

CHAPTER TWENTY-ONE

The descent into the market was quick and just as intoxicating as the first time. Finn was so used to being surrounded by magic that now that he was in a place where there was so little, the market was a little overwhelming.

Mila was right beside him, more comfortable than the first time, but also more aware of what she was seeing. She had a confidence she'd lacked the last time they were here, her shoulders back and her head up. She would nod to those who made eye contact and give a little smile to make them aware that she was in the know. It was amazing to Finn how the awoken Peabrains seemed to really take a shine to her, waving and smiling. One of the Peabrain food vendors handed her and Finn a paper plate with fair-style elephant ears covered in powdered sugar, saying welcome and waving off any payment. It seemed the Peabrain community was tight-knit here on the *Earth*.

Finn split his fried dough with Penny as they made their way through the market, looking for Garret and

Hermin. They found the two Huldu sitting at a bar that was open to the passing crowd, sipping large steins of what looked like dark beer.

"Hello, fellas," Finn greeted the two, giving each of them a friendly slap on the back.

Hermin, who was in mid-drink, chuffed some beer down his overalls, coughing and sputtering.

"Oh, shit. Sorry about that, Hermin. Maybe this will make you feel better." He placed the Helm of Awe on the counter between them.

Both gnomes' eyes went wide, and Garret picked up the helm, inspecting it. "Holy shit! You actually found the damn thing! I was just having a little wager with Hermin that you two wouldn't show up, or if you did, you would be empty-handed." He smiled at Mila. "Hello there."

"Hello." Mila waved and sat down beside Hermin at the counter. "Think that thing is worth a free round? I think Finn, Penny, and I could use a drink after the last couple of days we've had."

"Absolutely." Hermin waved to the bartender, a sleek-looking elf man in black leather pants and a deep V-neck. "Tony, another round, and three more for our friends here."

The elf nodded and began filling more steins.

"I was sure you three would find the helm," Hermin told them. "But I must admit, now that it's here, I can't believe it. I knew it would take a dwarf to find it. These old artifacts have a way of staying hidden."

"Actually," Finn nodded to Tony in thanks for his beer, "it was mostly Mila's and Penny's work. I was just the muscle when we needed it."

Mila grinned and took an embarrassed sip of beer. Penny, on the other hand, puffed out her chest and shot a victory flame into the sky, making everyone but Finn flinch back.

"Well, however you accomplished it, we are grateful." Garret finished his first stein, eyeing the dragon warily. "A deal is a deal. We can get you the parts you need. We didn't bring them here because they are a bit of a bother to transport, and to be honest, their value would make us a target. Not all of us are trained fighters."

"Speak for yourself, Garret." Hermin slapped his companion on the back. "I've learned a nice handful of spells in my centuries. I daresay we could handle ourselves if it came down to it."

"Actually, there's a problem," Finn confessed, cutting off their bravado. "The ship is no longer under my care. I had to trade it for the helm."

Garret and Hermin blinked confusedly at him. Hermin was the first to ask the obvious question.

"Why would you trade the ship for a helm that you would then trade for parts to fix the ship you just traded?"

Finn chuckled at the predicament. "Well, it's a little complicated. The helm was stolen by the Dark Star's minions, and they wanted the ship. They threatened to destroy the helm with her dark magic in downtown Denver if I didn't cooperate, so it was either give up the ship and save the city or keep the ship and... Well, you get the idea."

"Oh, my," Hermin mumbled, slightly slack-jawed. "She has the ability to use dark magic? After you mentioned the Dark Star last time we met, we did a little digging. It seems they have started a movement to carve out a nation for Magicals. We thought it was just talk, like it usually is, but if she is able to use dark magic, that changes things. We need to talk to our people. Would you be willing to help us with this problem?"

Finn nodded. "I was planning on asking you to help *me*, but either way works, I suppose. Since we don't need the parts for the ship anymore, I was hoping to trade a favor or two with you and your people."

"Absolutely," Garret chimed in right away. "This helm is worth more than a few favors, though."

"Don't get ahead of yourself," Finn warned. "I'm not sure what those favors might be just yet. You might be cursing my name in a few days."

Hermin and Garret chuckled.

"I doubt that," Hermin assured him for the both of them. "We had a few sections of the engines that badly needed parts replaced, but we couldn't get to them due to a lava flow blocking the way. With this, we can get down there and keep the old girl running for another thousand years."

"Wait," Mila held up a hand, her brows furrowed. "You're going to use that helmet to walk through lava? It's that powerful?"

"Oh, it's much more powerful than that. You could walk through a black hole with this thing on." Hermin held the rather plain bucket helmet up and rapped a knuckle on it, making it ring like a badly made bell.

"The Helm of Awe makes the wearer invincible," Finn explained, "but only for an hour, and only once per day."

"Then why don't we use it to fight this Dark Star person?" Mila asked.

Finn blew out a breath before answering. "Well, we could, but the problem is she knows its time constraints, so she could just wait us out. It sounds really powerful, and it is, but many wearers of the helm have fallen in battle when their time ran out. The helm is not a good crutch to rely on. It makes its wearers sloppy when the swords and spells start flying. Besides, the Huldu have a legitimate need for it, and it'll be safe in their keeping."

Garret wore a smile of pride at Finn's words about them being able to keep the helm safe. "Will you need help locating your ship? We have to stop them before they can get it off the ground. We can't have Peabrains running around like chickens with their heads cut off at the sight of an alien spaceship floating up into the sky." He glanced at Mila and reddened. "No offense."

Mila shrugged. "No offense taken. You're right, the world would lose its collective mind if the *Anthem* took off too close to the city."

"I think I have the location covered." Finn pulled a flat piece of stone from his jacket pocket, along with a small piece of purple chalk. He quickly sketched a crude compass with the chalk. "I attached a tracking spell to the hull of the ship a few days ago. This should lead us right to it."

Everyone leaned in, watching him work. Garret and Hermin in particular were glued to his every move.

"I never thought I would get a chance to see dwarven magic," Hermin muttered, not wanting to interrupt Finn's work but unable to not comment. "I had heard they didn't use bubbles like the rest of us, but I just didn't believe it."

"It's because dwarven magic is purely physical," Finn explained as he started drawing runes around the edge of the compass's circle. "We can't teleport or send messages or any of that fancy stuff. Our magic is about attaching power to things or channeling things through ourselves with power. It's why my people are the best artificers, and also why it's so difficult for other races to figure out how to use those artifacts." He held out the flat stone and admired his work. "There. Now I just need to power it up, and it will connect to the ship."

He pulled the stone close to his lips and began to speak words of power into it. He had practiced enough that he knew no one could hear the words, no matter how hard they tried. After a few seconds, the chalk and stone both began to glow deep purple and the air filled with the fresh scent of pine.

Finn held the stone out so everyone could see it. The dial was now moving as if it were a real needle and not just a chalk drawing.

Mila and the others let out a little gasp when the dial spun in a circle, then sparked green and let off a small plume of smoke.

"Chi seetri?" Penny asked, raising an eye ridge.

"Yes, I did the runes in the correct order," Finn growled, shaking the stone as if it were a malfunctioning piece of tech. "You saw what I had. It was right. The compass just didn't have anything to connect to."

"They must have found your marker on the ship," Hermin suggested.

"It was a dwarven mark, though," Garret said with a shake of his head. "They would need someone who could find dwarven markings, and Finn is the only dwarf on this ship."

"Jeff." Mila sighed, looking at Finn, who nodded. "He said he could find and activate dwarven artifacts in his note. They must be using him."

"Qree chi shitri. Chits?" Penny patted Mila on the shoulder from her place on the counter.

"She's right." Finn grinned. "That means Jeff is with the ship. If we can find it, that puts us one step closer to saving him as well. Boys, it looks like we'll need some help finding the ship after all. Think you can?"

Garret puffed up at the challenge. "Hell, yes, we can! We will have its location in no time."

Hermin swirled his finger, spitting out a stream of golden light that formed a bubble on the counter. It popped, leaving behind a small stack of business cards with Hermin's name on them.

"Here, take these. They will be the best way to reach us, and I can use the cards to find you and send messages back. Just write on the card and toss it into the air. They'll find me wherever I am. We'll be in touch soon."

They all said their goodbyes, and the two gnomes hurried off into the crowd.

Finn pulled the box of Charleston Chews from his jacket and offered one to Mila as they watched them go.

"No, thanks. I could use a real meal, though. I haven't eaten in a while." Mila's stomach growled just then as if to prove the point.

"Come on." Finn stood, popping a few of the chews into his mouth. "Let's head back to your place. I'll make us something."

"You can cook, too?" Mila fanned her face with an open hand. "Be still, my heart."

Finn rolled his eyes and parted the crowd with his large body as he stepped onto the walkway between booths. "Wait until you taste my food."

"Is it good?" Mila asked Penny, who was draped over Finn's shoulder and looking at her.

Penny nodded vigorously, then took a bite of a chew she had nabbed on her way up from the counter.

CHAPTER TWENTY-TWO

At Mila's apartment, Finn had found the ingredients for several meals he could make, but he decided on a simple pasta dish that would only take twenty minutes or so to prepare. A few cans of tomatoes and mushrooms, along with a chopped onion and generous amounts of spices, made a hearty sauce he put over pasta cooked in water "as salty as the sea." A sprinkling of cheese, and they had themselves a delicious dish.

Mila opened a bottle of red wine and poured two glasses, then a third one in a small tumbler for Penny.

They sat at the counter on stools and ate in silence. Finn hadn't realized how hungry he was until the first bite, then it was nearly a race to see who would finish their bowl first. Each of them huffed and slurped down the hot meal, and decided to fill their bowls with seconds.

"Holy shit, Finn," Mila exclaimed after eating half her second bowl. "Where did you learn to make Italian food like this? I had no idea food made with canned goods could be so good."

"What's Italian food?" he asked, wiping his mustache with a paper towel before going in for another bite.

"You know, food from Italy. It's a place in Europe."

He frowned and looked down at the bowl of pasta in front of him. "This is a traditional Pixie dish. I didn't know you guys had anything like it on the *Earth*. Now I feel bad that I didn't make something you haven't had before."

Mila laughed. "Don't feel bad! It's really good. The best I can do is add an egg to instant ramen to make it fancy."

"What's 'ramen?'" Finn asked, taking another bite.

Mila's fork stopped halfway to her mouth and she stared wide-eyed at him. "You don't know what ramen is? Oh, my God. It's only the most delicious food ever created. Holy shit, I can't believe I get to take you out for your first bowl of ramen. This is better than meeting someone who's never seen *Star Wars* or *Firefly*."

The blank look on Finn's face made her gasp.

"Have you not seen *Star Wars* or *Firefly*?!"

He shook his head. "Never even heard of them. I only saw what I was able to record from deep space. I must have missed those."

"Holy shit." She smiled so wide, he thought she was going to pull a muscle. "We are going to have the best time when we get back. Two marathons and ramen for days. Oh, man, I can't fucking wait!"

Finn and Penny exchanged looks, nervous smiles on their faces. Mila was really excited, which meant they were going to have to be excited, even if the shows sucked. So far, though, her taste had lined up with his, so he wasn't too worried. Still, it was a lot of pressure.

Finn finished eating first and took his bowl to the sink,

then started rummaging through the cupboards, looking for something to put the leftovers in. He found some clear plastic containers with lids that would be perfect. When he stood back up, Mila was coming around the island with her and Penny's bowls. She turned on the water and began washing up.

He put the rest of the pasta in the container and poured the thick sauce on top. He had to shake the container to get the pasta to settle enough to get the lid on properly. He had to shimmy around Mila, who was on the third bowl, the clean ones in the drying rack. Opening the refrigerator, he found a spot for the container, then wrote a little note on a sticky piece of paper on the counter that said, Danica, please help yourself and stuck it to the lid.

Mila had grabbed the pots and was starting on them.

"You don't have to do that," Finn said, stepping up beside her. "I made the mess, I can clean it up."

She hip-checked him, which made her stumble to the side more than him when their difference in body weight came into play. "Get out of here. Everyone knows that if you cook, someone else cleans. Go away. I can't clean properly with you looming over me," she joked, hitting him with a squirt from the spout and making him jump back.

"Okay. I never like the cleaning up part anyway," he said, his hands up in surrender as he backed up to lean on the counter and watch her.

"Shi thri!" Penny protested, hopping from the table to the counter beside the sink.

"Hey, I heard that." Finn gave her a narrow-eyed look. "I didn't see you cleaning up after I made dinner on the *Anthem*, either."

215

Penny had the good sense to look chagrined.

Mila laughed. "It's fine. I don't mind cleaning as long as you keep on cooking. That was one of the best meals I've had in a while. It'll be nice having someone around who can cook. Danica and I are helpless in the kitchen."

Finn watched her work, scrubbing and humming some tune he had never heard. He caught what she said, although he was sure she hadn't. She seemed to think he would be staying with her for at least the foreseeable future. The half-smile on Penny's face told him she had caught it as well.

Would that be a bad thing? Not in his mind, and Penny seemed to like it here, but wherever he went, he seemed to bring trouble along with him, and the last thing he wanted was to get Mila or Danica hurt. Knowing Mila, she would probably just follow him anyway, even if he told her not to. She didn't take well to being told what she could and couldn't do, which was one of the things he liked about her.

The universe will provide.

It was a saying he tried to live by, and so far, it hadn't let him down. Sure, there were thin times, and times when he wasn't sure he and Penny were going to make it, but they always did. Maybe Mila was how the universe was providing for him now.

Finn frowned. It seemed a little one-sided to him. She wasn't getting nearly the same thing out of their meeting that he was. Then again, what did he know? Maybe this was exactly what she needed.

He opened his mouth to broach the subject with her when the door burst open, and a sweating and out of breath Danica stumbled into the room. Finn had Fragar half out of its holster before he realized she wasn't in danger.

She wore a pair of white leggings and a matching sports bra, along with running shoes. She gave them a big smile and pulled her earbuds out.

"Hey, guys," she said between gulping breaths. "I thought you would still be gone." She opened the fridge and took out a water bottle, downing half of it before coming up for air. "How did the swap meet go?"

Mila dried the last spoon and put it in the drawer. "As well as could be expected, when it comes to losing the only interstellar spaceship on the planet. The knight guy was a real asshole about the whole thing, so that was fun. How about you? I see you got a run in."

Danica took a paper towel and wiped the sweat from her face and arms. "Yeah. After you guys left, I tried to sit around and not worry, but that didn't go well, so I decided to go for a run. Then I stopped back here, and you weren't home, so I went back out for another one. Pretty sure I hit thirty miles today."

"You ran a marathon and some because you were worried?" Mila asked, her eyes going wide. "Damn, girl. I didn't know you had it in you."

She shrugged and opened the fridge, then took out the pasta and read the note on top. "Aw, thanks, guys. This looks delish." She opened the microwave and put the container in for a minute to take the chill off. "Thirty miles isn't all that far for a wood elf. I could probably do a hundred without much trouble."

"Wait, I thought you were a high elf?" Finn cut in, handing her a fork.

"Thanks. No, I'm a wood elf. I dye my hair." She smiled and took a bite. "Oh, man, this is really good. Where's it from?"

"The cupboard." Mila laughed. "Finn made it."

Danica looked at him, her eyes nearly tearing up. "Please stay with us forever. You can have my room. I'll sleep on the floor, as long as you make food like this every day."

Finn smiled and was about to answer when a breeze blew the balcony door open. They all turned and saw a bubble about a foot across come floating in and cross the room toward them. When it reached the halfway point, it burst and a note fell out.

"Wow, Hermin and Garret work fast." Finn walked over and picked up the folded piece of paper and gave it a read. "Looks like they found the *Anthem* and are willing to transport us there if we want. Hermin is waiting at the entrance to the market."

"Oh, shit. I didn't think this was going down tonight." Mila pushed off the counter and headed for her room.

"Where are you going?" Finn asked, watching her go.

She plucked at the gray t-shirt she had been wearing all day. "To change. If we're going to be sneaking around, I should probably not wear a short-sleeved V-neck shirt. Don't you have combat pants or something?"

Finn smiled. "Yeah. I do. They're whatever I happen to be wearing when combat starts."

Mila rolled her eyes but laughed. "Well, I'm going to prepare. Give me a minute."

Finn decided she might have a point and went to the leather bag he had brought his and Penny's things in. He rummaged until he found the black cargo pants he had stuffed into the bottom, and undid his belt buckle. He was down to his tight black boxer briefs when he heard Danica's fork scrape her bowl. Turning, he saw her leaning on the counter, watching him change.

She waved the fork at him. "Don't stop on my account. I'm just enjoying dinner and a show over here."

Finn chuckled and changed, keeping the black t-shirt and harness on and pulling on his black leather jacket once the cargo pants were secured with his belt. Mila came out of her room dressed similarly, except she wore black tights and combat boots that made her feet look about two sizes too big. She finished the look with a form-fitting hoodie and a black turtleneck underneath.

"Wow, you weren't kidding about wanting to sneak around. You look like a goth chick with a YouTube channel," Danica joked.

"Har har." Mila put her hands on her hips, taking the jab with ease. "Actually, these boots were from my high school days. I was all edgy and stuff, or at least, my mom thought I was."

"Unlike undergrad, when you got that tramp stamp?" Danica's eyes nearly glowed with mirth.

"Hey!" Mila pointed a finger at her roommate's face. "We don't talk about the tramp stamp."

"What's a tramp—"

Finn was cut off by Mila's other hand pointing at him.

"I said we don't talk about it! Now let's go. I want to get there before Jeff is taken to some other location."

That sobered Finn right up. He was so used to adventure that he often forgot there were real consequences for some people involved.

"Right. Let's go. Danica, hold down the fort. We'll be back before you know it." He shot her a smile as he passed and opened the door for Mila.

"Sure thing, guys." Danica waved in an overly stiff manner. "Have fun storming the castle."

"We're not storming a castle." He gave her a confused look.

She sighed. "It's from a movie. Never mind."

Mila shook her head as she passed. "How have you never seen *The Princess Bride?*"

"I'm from another planet. By the way, what's a goth?" he asked as he closed the door.

CHAPTER TWENTY-THREE

Finn and Mila walked down the alley leading to the market. Night had fallen, and the sounds of the city were muffled between the brick buildings. Despite the relative quiet of the alley, Hermin was showing no sign that he had heard them approach as he stared down the opposite way. Finn cleared his throat when they were a few paces away, making the short gnome nearly jump out of his skin.

Hermin pressed a hand to his chest and gasped for breath. "Oh, my heart. Dear gods, why did you sneak up on me like that? I thought you were the Dark Star's people."

"Sorry, Hermin," Finn said gently. "We didn't mean to scare you. To be honest, though, we weren't being particularly quiet. Why would you think the Dark Star's people would know you were here?"

Hermin got himself under control, but he continued to look down the alley to be sure they were alone. "It turns out a lot of people know who this Dark Star is and are secretly rooting for her. There seems to be a large portion of the magical community that doesn't want to spend the rest of their years in hiding because the Peabrains are having memory problems. Garret and I might have been a little sloppy in our search at first and alerted some people that we were looking for her."

Now Finn was on edge. He hadn't realized just how deep the Dark Star had her talons.

"Right. Well, then we should get out of here and let you get back to...wherever you live. How far is the *Anthem*?" he asked.

Hermin grunted. "Just about as far as you can get. It took quite a few scrying spells to find, and we had friends double-check our work just to be sure. The whole Huldu community came together on this one, and now they're keeping a close eye on what happens. The Dark Star transported the ship to an ice cave in Antarctica. I would have said it was impossible for one person to do that, but there it is."

"Antarctica?" Mila exclaimed. "You have got to be kidding me. I'm not dressed for that."

"Don't worry," Hermin reassured her, pulling two vials from his overalls and handing one to each of them. "I figured you might need assistance with that. Here are some potions for cold resistance. They will give you a good eight hours before you need to find shelter. Sorry, I couldn't find anyone who knew the proper recipe for dragons."

"Chi, chi." Penny waved him off, assuring him that she would be fine. She sucked in a breath and puffed out her cheeks as if she were blowing fire with her mouth closed.

Finn felt the waves of heat start to radiate off of her and

gave her a pat. "She'll be fine," he confirmed. He opened the vial and downed the light blue liquid. Then he looked at Mila, who was hesitating. "Bottoms up. Don't worry, it tastes like cinnamon."

She smiled and unstopped hers before taking a swig.

Finn quickly reached over and tilted it up so she had to drink the whole thing. "You need to take it all at once or it won't work. Sorry, should have warned you."

She gulped it down, then smacked her lips. "That's actually pretty good. Whoa, I can feel it warming my belly. Holy shit, that's amazing. It's like drinking a bottle of whiskey without getting drunk."

"You two ready?" Hermin asked, glancing over his shoulder. "I'm going to put you as far from the ship as I can while still keeping you in the cave."

"Shirit, shee. Churist," Penny protested, making Hermin's eyebrows furrow in confusion.

"She's right." Finn translated, "Put us as close to the ship as you can. That way, if there are guards, there will be less chance of them seeing us, since we'll be behind them. Plus, I can get us in through any of the *Anthem's* access hatches, so we won't be out in the open for long."

Hermin nodded. "Good thinking. Okay, ready?"

Finn and Mila held hands and nodded.

"Here we go."

Hermin began to blow a bubble from his mouth that grew until it was seven or eight feet tall and just touched the ground. There was a rainbow sheen to its surface, and the alley was filled with the smell of fresh-cut cucumber as Hermin's magic flowed from him.

He sucked in a breath and motioned for them to step inside. "Quickly, now."

Finn stepped forward, thinking he would have to pull Mila into the strange magical structure, but he was surprised to see that she was one step ahead of him and pulling *him* forward. He passed through the bubble's surface and the alley winked out of existence, to be replaced by the rough surface of the *Anthem*.

Finn immediately dropped into a crouch and spun to get a quick look at their surroundings. Mila followed suit, surprisingly graceful in her movements, considering she had never infiltrated enemy territory before.

The cave was huge and obviously not natural. It looked like someone had melted out a thousand feet of ice with a mini sun. The walls were smooth and featureless, reflecting the lights set up around the ship. The ice here was so old it was more green than blue or white. Finn's dwarven senses told him the ceiling of the cave was only a few yards thick—strong enough to hold its own weight, but thin enough that the *Anthem* would have no problems breaking through.

He didn't see any guards, but they could only see half the cave, being so close to the ship.

"Hear anything?" he whispered.

"No, just dripping water," Mila confirmed.

"Penny, go up and take a look, then meet us at access hatch four."

Penny nodded and flapped her wings silently, shooting up and over the huge asteroid.

"Come on." Finn motioned for Mila to follow.

They moved in a crouched run around the base of the

ship until they came to landing strut that had been deployed to keep the round rock stable while on the ground. Finn moved around it and admired that Mila did the same in a smooth motion. She was good at this.

They continued quickly until Finn put up a hand and squatted again, stopping their progress.

Mila leaned in and whispered, tickling his ear, "Did you hear something?"

A shiver ran down his spine but he resisted the urge to scratch his earlobe. "No, we're waiting for Penny." He touched the rocky surface. "The hatch is right here."

She stared at the *Anthem* for a few seconds before whispering, "How can you tell?"

Finn looked at her like she was crazy, then looked at the ship, his brow furrowed. "I don't know, I just can. It looks like a door to me."

A bubble appeared right between them, making Mila suck in a breath and put her hands up to guard her face. The small bubble popped, and a note drifted to the ground between them. Finn picked it up with his left hand, having grabbed Fragar out of reflex with his right, and unfolded the note.

"It's from Hermin. He says the Huldu have decided that if the *Anthem* takes off, they will have to destroy her. He says the Peabrains will almost certainly see it, and they can't risk it."

"What if we're on the ship?" Mila asked, leaning in so she could read the note as well.

"I guess that didn't factor into their decision. I would say let's not be on it if it's going to take off."

"So, how do we stop it?" She wrapped her hand around

his arm to keep steady in their crouched position, and Finn didn't mind at all.

"I say we go for the engines. The *Anthem* has been on her last legs for…well, a long time. It shouldn't be too hard to break a few things in the engine room to get her to give up the ghost."

Penny swooped around the ship, tooting a flame to signal the all-clear, then landed on his shoulder.

"Nice." He bumped fists with her as she settled on his shoulder.

Mila reached up and mimicked Finn, receiving a fist bump of her own that made Finn smile.

"Okay, let's do this," he said. "You have your armor on and Gram at the ready?"

Mila pulled her turtleneck down until the chainmail showed, then reached in her hoodie's pocket and pulled out the gold hilt of Gram. "Ready."

Finn pressed a hand to the stone and a panel lit up. Recognizing him, the ship opened the air-tight seal of access door four with a hiss, then swung inward. The opening was small, but Finn could make it if he turned his shoulders sideways and pushed hard with his feet. He wiggled until his right arm was inside the ship, then he pulled himself the rest of the way in.

He fell to the grated floor of an access walkway between the main cargo hold and water storage. He nearly cursed when he saw Mila's small frame step through the door without having to do much in the way of squeezing.

Instead, he smiled at her. "That's got to be nice."

"What does?" Mila asked, brushing frost off her pants.

"Fitting through spaces." He chuckled. "I've been over

six feet tall since I was ten. Not a lot of time to enjoy being small." He stood up and had to duck so he didn't hit his head on a pipe from the water tank.

"Being small has its advantages, but so does being big," she argued. "Like the fact that you can kick ten sorts of ass without worrying too much about it. That must be nice."

"My father once told me that the difference between a peaceful man and a helpless man was that a peaceful man could kill but didn't, and a helpless man couldn't kill in the first place."

Mila cocked her head to the side and furrowed her brow. "That seems a little all-or-nothing."

"Yeah, my dad is a bit of an asshole," he agreed, leading the way down the access tunnel. "But it was a good reminder that most people will put you in a category right off the bat. I've seen a lot of guys get their asses kicked by smaller foes because they forgot the simple fact that being badass has nothing to do with size or, to some degree, skill. It has to do with wanting to win and knowing how far you're willing to go to get that victory."

"Okay, but that still doesn't mean I can kick the same amount of ass as you can," she reasoned.

Finn slowed down as they came to a T intersection. "Which way is the engine room?"

Penny pointed to the left and rolled her eyes. "Squee shir?"

"Yes, this is my ship," Finn said with a huff. "You know I don't spend much time down here in the access tunnels. And don't even say that it shows; you're not funny. It's just mean at some point."

Penny chuckled and patted him on the head as he turned left and continued.

"Back to the topic at hand. You may not be able to kick the quantity of ass I can, but you sure kick quality ass. No one will see you coming. Guys underestimate smaller foes."

He led them up a series of ladders and more walkways while Mila considered his words. Eventually, he stopped at a hatch in the floor of the tunnel.

"Here we are. The heart of the ship. I say we slip in, pull a few fuses, break a couple of valves, and then we can take our time to find that one-eyed bastard and set him straight."

Penny nodded along with Mila, who pulled Gram out but didn't activate it.

Finn carefully pulled the hatch in the walkway open, careful not to make any noise.

He needn't have bothered. The room a dozen feet below was full of Kashgar, but each was working on a system and chatting excitedly with one another.

"I can't believe we're going to finally see our homeworld."

"Won't the Dark Star be pissed we're taking the ship?"

"Who cares? We'll be so far away, she won't be able to do anything."

"I hope she doesn't find out."

"Lithor really stuck his neck out for us. I can't believe he's going against…"

Finn slowly closed the hatch and frowned at Mila. "Well, that was unexpected."

"The fact that Lithor is stealing the ship from his boss?"

"No." Finn swallowed. "The fact that the engines have

never looked so clean and been in such good working order."

"Okay, but how does that change the plan?" Mila asked, her grip on Gram making her knuckles white.

Finn sighed. "Well, first off, those are basically civilians who are just trying to get to a home that they've never seen. I don't like the idea of slaughtering mechanics. But more importantly, they actually fixed so much stuff that the backups are working. I don't think we can do enough damage before they overwhelm us."

"Shir chi shee," Penny suggested.

"Yeah, we're going to have to take care of this from the bridge. I'm betting that's where Lithor is anyway." Finn chewed the inside of his cheek while he thought. "Problem with that is I can't fit through the vent shafts to get there unnoticed. I'm going to have to fight my way through." He paused for a second, then looked at Mila. "You, on the other hand, can fit just fine." He flashed her a smile. "See? Being small pays off."

She huffed a laugh. "Okay, so what's the plan?"

"Come on. We need to find the access shaft to the bridge and do a little more scouting." He grabbed the next ladder and began to climb, Mila right behind him.

Five minutes later, they were crouching over the closest access panel to the bridge that Finn could get to. A little farther down, the tunnel narrowed enough that he simply couldn't fit.

"You need to go that way until you come to a vent like this one. That will look down onto the bridge," Finn whispered.

They needed to be quiet because just below them were

a dozen guards filling the hallway to the bridge. Most of them were sitting on crates and chatting, but each of them had a weapon close at hand and obviously knew how to use it.

"What do I do once I'm there?"

Mila was shaking slightly, and not from the cool air flowing through the vents, Finn guessed.

"Just wait for me and Penny to get in there, then you can drop down behind them and hit the two red buttons on the main console. They're the emergency shutdown for the engines. It'll take them an hour to get them back up and running. By then, we should have the situation under control. The guards below Lithor and us are their only combatants, so the rest should give up pretty easily once we take care of those guys."

"Okay, I can do that." She peered down through the grate at the dozen armed Kashgar. "Are you two going to be okay?"

Finn gave her a smile. "We've faced worse. We'll be fine. Just wish me luck."

She moved suddenly, throwing her arms around his neck and kissing him full on the lips.

Finn's eyes widened in surprise, but before he could kiss her back, she pulled away.

"Good luck," she whispered and scurried off down the narrowing vent.

"What the fuck?" Finn said. He touched his lips, then smiled.

Penny slapped him on the back of the head. "Chi shi?"

"I know I didn't kiss her back. I was shocked she did it at all!" He grinned. "That's all the more motivation to get through this and show her what a proper kiss from a dwarf is like."

Penny rolled her eyes but nodded. She was ready.

Finn griped Fragar and whispered the power word before kicking the grate open and dropping into the passage.

CHAPTER TWENTY-FOUR

Finn dropped to the deck and roared. The closest Kashgar tumbled backward over the crate he had been sitting on, a look of absolute fear plastered on his face. The three behind him, while shocked, were quicker on the uptake, and snapped open their riot batons, electricity crackling down their lengths as the figures holding them charged.

Finn felt his blood begin to boil as he let his berserker rage flow free. He leapt forward, tackling all three charging men with his arms open wide. Two of the electrically charged batons slapped against his back, making the muscles tense and spasm, but his momentum was enough to take all three to the ground. He pushed up and punched the man in the middle hard enough that his head bounced off the deck plating, knocking him out cold.

The Kashgar on the right swung his baton again, hitting Finn in the arm and numbing it, but not enough to keep the dwarf from bashing the flat of Fragar's blade into the attacker's nose, sending out a spray of blood. The third man's head nearly got chopped in half, but as Finn swung his axe, he was hit in the chest by a small, fast-moving bubble that exploded and sent him flying backward off the men under him.

He saw Penny swoop from the vent and keep close to the ceiling, heading further down the corridor, before he smashed into the wall and fell to the floor. Finn was on his feet in the blink of an eye, running full speed back into the fray, his chest throbbing, but only dully aware of it in the back of his mind.

The Kashgar that had fallen off his crate was now up and began unloading a pistol in Finn's direction. Luckily, fear made for bad aim, and Finn was able to get close enough to swing Fragar and take one of the man's arms off before he could be hit.

Launching himself into the air, Finn planted a knee into the face of the man he had been blown off of, and a crunching sound let Finn know that the man wouldn't be getting back up any time soon.

The ringing sound of rushing blood muted the sounds around him, but a scream made Finn focus on the back line of the quickly recovering guards. He saw one of the casters holding his hands to his face, and blood was oozing out from where Penny had raked her talons over exposed flesh. A burst of flame caught another's arm on fire, and he fell into the man beside him.

Figuring Penny had the back line busy for the moment, Finn found closer targets.

Four Kashgar were pulling up rifles, while the remaining two held out their hands and began to cast offensive spells.

Finn threw Fragar at the closest man with a rifle, burying the blade in his chest and knocking him into the man behind him, sending both to the ground, one dead and the other tangled in his compatriot's body. The two casters let loose a flurry of small bubbles that shot past the two remaining riflemen and began exploding against Finn's arms and chest. He roared again, his bloodlust powering him through the barrage, but not without taking serious damage.

His shirt and flesh were torn and blasted away in small chunks, sending splashes of blood onto the walls and Kashgar alike, but Finn kept on coming, his boots pounding on the deck plates in an inevitable drumbeat of war.

"*Lamh meatailt.*"

Finn's voice was hoarse, but the words rang true as the corridor filled with the smell of pine. The floor glowed purple before it warped and stretched, forming a hand that grasped one of the caster's legs at the thigh and clamped down hard enough that the bone broke before it yanked him down and locked into place, becoming inanimate once again.

"*Gunna salainn.*"

Finn's second spell blasted large salt crystals from his palm and into the chest of the other caster, the impact picking him up and throwing him against the closed doors to the bridge.

The two remaining riflemen opened up at point-blank range. Finn was able to get close enough to grab the barrel of one of the rifles and yank it from the Kashgar's hand, pulling the unbalanced man into the line of fire of the other rifleman, who put several rounds into his friend's back before he let go of the trigger.

Finn used the rifle in his hand like a club and broke the jaw of the last rifleman with a swing that would have made Babe Ruth jealous.

Penny had taken out the three in the back with either flame or talon, or both, and was now flapping her wings and closing in on him.

The blood rage was making him see nothing but red, and his leg hurt like it had caught fire and was being dipped in acid at the same time. He looked down, barely registering that he had been shot three times in the left leg and was bleeding from a dozen or more burned craters pockmarking his chest and arms. The berserker rage gave him unnatural stamina and strength, but even that had a limit.

Dropping to one knee, Finn reached around to the back of his harness and fished out one of the healing potions, but his fingers were too numb to pull the stopper, and he fell forward, the vial spinning down the corridor. He blinked, but his vision was darkening from red to black. He did his best to get up but was only able to roll over onto his back and stare up into the lights.

The last thought he had before the blackness overtook him was that the damn Kashgar had even fixed the flickering lights in the hall.

Mila crawled through the tight vent, not knowing how far she had to go but determined to be there in time. Her elbows scraped along, getting abrasions even through her hoodie. She could barely move, but she needed to do so quietly, or she'd be found out early. Stubbornly, she made steady, slow progress.

Her lips still tingled from where Finn's beard had rubbed against them, a constant reminder of her impetuous action. Now that she had time to think about it, she wasn't sure it had been the right move at all. They barely knew each other, and he wasn't even human. Though, technically, she was a Peabrain, but she still wasn't entirely sure what that meant. The last thing she wanted was to scare Finn off as she tended to do with most guys.

She hadn't been paying attention to how far she had come until a small furry gray spider came rushing at her, waving its little front legs in warning.

She stopped moving and cocked her head at the little guy, who paused a few feet in front of her, waving her off. The spider's behavior reminded her of the moth from her room before the four men attacked the condo.

"What is it?" she asked him.

She had received warnings from insects throughout her life, but she had never seen a spider act so directly, obviously trying to communicate.

The little spider pointed to her right with both arms. She turned her head to see what he was on about and sucked in a sharp breath.

On the side of the vent was a mark that she could just make out when she looked at it from the corner of her eye. She recognized it as magical, but if she tried to look directly at it, it faded from her view. She swept her eyes across it a few times and caught glimpses, but that was it.

"I can sort of see it, but I don't know what to do about it. Hell, I don't even know what it is." She turned back to the little spider, who was now dancing back and forth. "How am I supposed to avoid whatever it is?"

She leaned in to see if the spider was trying to signal something more complicated, but it just stared at her, swaying.

She sighed and tried to think of what Finn would do. She stopped that line of thinking when she realized he would probably just ignore it.

Instead, she thought about what Penny would do. That didn't lead anywhere for the opposite reason; Penny was far too advanced with magic for Mila to try to emulate.

An idea of her own popped into her head, and she wiggled until she could get her hand into the pocket of her tights. She had a receipt in there from when they had gotten gas on the way back from an earlier trip to the *Anthem.*

She struggled to move well enough to fish it out, but she finally managed, after scraping her arm on an exposed screw. She wadded the receipt into a tight little ball, and using only her wrist and fingers, threw it at the mark— which turned out to be much harder to do when she couldn't look at it straight on. On her third attempt, the small wad of paper hit.

The mark flashed brightly for a second before discharging a blue flame that vaporized the ball of paper before it hit the ground.

Mila's eyes were wide with fear, and she shook when she realized what that spell would have done to her. She glanced at the wall, sweeping her eyes back and forth, but saw no sign of the mark. Either it was a one-time-use spell, or she was too frightened to see it anymore.

She decided that once this was all over, she was going to start taking magic lessons from Danica and Penny. Right after she learned Penny's language, if that was even possible.

She glanced down at the spider, who was doing a victory dance, and smiled. "Thanks, little buddy. Was that the only one, or are there more?"

The spider waggled back and forth, which she somehow knew meant there were no more traps.

She moved her hand forward, extending a finger until it was within arm's reach for the spider. "Put 'er there, little guy. You just saved my bacon."

The spider fist-bumped her before running back down the vent.

"Well, that was cool," she said to herself, starting to shinny forward again. "Guess I have a little guardian angel in here with me."

Her confidence was at an all-time high as she inched forward, right up until the point that the bottom of the vent was torn out from under her, and she fell the ten feet to the floor of the bridge.

She would have groaned from the impact, but the wind had been knocked out of her. She struggled as she tried to get up. A hand reached down and grabbed her by the collar, lifting her into the air as if she weighed nothing. She blinked tears from her eyes and stared into the face of Lithor, his one good eye narrowed and full of contempt.

"You think you can sneak up on me after setting off one of my traps? How stupid do you think I am?" He shook her as if she were a puppy who had pissed in his shoe. "Now, where is that giant buffoon you're so fond of?"

Mila was about to spit in his face and tell him to go fuck himself when she was interrupted by automatic gunfire coming from beyond the door. Then there was the sound of someone hitting the metal doors hard and sliding down them.

She and Lithor stared at the sealed hatch, waiting for something to happen, but there was just silence.

Lithor sneered as he turned back to her. "Looks like he met some high-speed lead. It's a shame, really. I was hoping to slit your throat in front of him, but I'll just have to save you for later." He pulled a wicked curved knife from his belt and lifted it to her throat.

"Sir! Should I check to see that the men are all right?" someone behind Mila said, alerting her that there were others on the bridge with them.

Lithor sighed and ground his teeth but looked past Mila and addressed the other. "Not yet. Get us moving. We need to get out of here before the Mistress finds out we've moved up the launch. She would not take kindly to us stealing her new ship."

The ship began to hum from deep within its bowels, a feeling of power not unlike the one Mila got from her Hellcat when she punched the gas and rocketed down the highway.

Lithor glanced to the left, distracted by movement and wanting to see the launch from the viewscreen, even though he still held the curve of the blade to her throat. She could make out from the corner of her eye that the ship was rising through the ice cave and picking up speed.

A few seconds later, the *Anthem* shuddered, and huge chunks of ice began to rain down as they broke through the ceiling. The bright, clear day nearly blinded her, even making Lithor blink a few times.

When he saw they were clear of the cave, he turned back to her, his smile evil and slightly too big. "Goodbye, little mouse. You have been a pain in my side for far too—"

The double metal doors screeched and groaned, warping in their frame and opening a hole in their middle. An axe came hurtling through the gap and took the pilot in the back. He slumped and landed on the throttle controls, jamming them forward.

The ship lurched as its speed increased exponentially.

CHAPTER TWENTY-FIVE

Finn sucked in a breath, then began to choke on the liquid in his mouth. He felt a small hand holding his forehead down and resisted the urge to fight it.

"Shiri chiri," Penny cooed, urging him to drink.

He gulped down the rest of the vial she held to his lips and felt the magic doing its work. He also knew it wasn't going to be enough for his dwarven body and fished out the second healing potion. Penny stepped back, and he sat up to down the contents.

He felt the small craters on his torso and arms closing, but slower than he would have liked. He was still covered in blood, but at least he was alive, and in a few minutes, he would be fully healed and ready to face Lithor.

"Thanks, Penny." He gave her little arm a squeeze. "Once again, you saved my life."

She shrugged like it was no big deal and puffed a smoke ring from her nostril, but she was smiling with a touch of pride.

That was when the *Anthem* powered up her engines and took off.

The ship was well designed, and the movements were slight compared to the forces in play, but Finn knew those movements better than anyone.

"Oh, shit."

He scrambled to his feet and raced to the bridge's double doors. He pressed his hand to the control panel, but nothing happened.

He tried again, but still nothing.

"Shit. They've locked us out and changed the codes."

"Chi squir?" Penny suggested, flapping up next to him.

"No time to go around. I'll have to break the doors down. Stand back."

He took a couple of steps back, then pulled Fragar from the chest of the rifleman he had thrown it into and held his free hand toward the door.

"Fosgailte arsa mi."

The door began to glow with purple light, and bubbled slightly, as if it were heating up. When the magic had its hold on the door, Finn balled his fist and jerked his hand to the side.

A screeching noise filled the passageway and the door warped and twisted, finally splitting open in the middle, making a hole large enough for him to fit through.

He saw someone at the controls of the ship, and reacted, throwing Fragar as hard as he could. The axe buried itself in the man's back, but when he fell forward, the ship sped up, making Finn stumble.

"Fuck. Didn't think that one through," he admonished himself before charging for the gap.

"Watch out!" he heard Mila scream as he was about to go through the opening.

Unable to change his momentum and stop, he instead dove for the bottom of the opening and felt the hairs on the back of his neck stand on end as a bubble passed over him, right where he would have come through. It exploded on the bulkhead. The blast sent him tumbling, but he managed to roll to his feet just in time to see Lithor, holding Mila by the collar, level a curved blade at his face. The magic was already gathering, and he was not able to scramble out of the way.

Suddenly, the golden blade of Gram shot through the material of Mila's hoodie, and stabbed Lithor in the stomach. The mage screamed and threw her to the ground, turning his blade toward her and loosing the spell that had been meant for Finn.

A bubble six inches across flew from the dagger's tip and slammed into her chest, exploding and sending her flying back to smash into the wall and crumple to the floor.

Penny shot past Finn and Lithor, landing beside Mila.

Finn felt his rage take him, but glancing out the viewscreen, he could see hundreds of tiny bubbles flying up from the ground and attaching themselves to the hull of the *Anthem*. The Huldu were staying true to their word. His ship wouldn't last another minute before they set those bubbles off and destroyed it.

Another spell shot from Lithor's dagger, making Finn dive to the side. He rolled up next to the pilot's chair and pulled Fragar free, using the flat of the blade to deflect the next incoming spell. It ricocheted off and blew the navigation console to scrap.

Finn knew they had one chance to get out, and turned to the main console, his eyes flickering over the controls. Finding the button he was looking for, he slapped it. A door on the other side of the bridge, close to Penny and Mila, slid open, revealing three bucket seats with harnesses. Finn took a bubble to his side for his trouble, blowing fresh skin and fabric away, and making him growl in pain. Another spell hit him in the chest, knocking the wind out of him and opening a new wound.

Finn dropped to his knees, the pain overwhelming him. He saw Lithor's feet step in close, and felt the tip of the dagger hook under his chin, making him look up into the one-eyed man's face. Movement behind the Kashgar caught Finn's eye, but he kept his focus on Lithor.

"How dare you come onto *my* ship and kill my people? I told you what I would do if you came back. Looks like I'll have to find someone else to kill in front of you since that fucking bitch went down like the helpless Peabrain she was."

Finn smiled up at him. He could taste the blood on his teeth and his strength was bleeding out of his chest, but it was all he could do to not laugh. He saw a flash of silver and gold behind the Kashgar.

"That's some bold talk for a one-eyed fat man," Finn said, grinning at the confused look on Lithor's face. "Oh, and just to be clear, Mila's peaceful, not helpless."

"What the fuck is that supposed to—"

Gram's gold blade of sliced cleanly through Lithor's neck, leaving his head on his shoulders, but no longer attached. Lithor's mouth opened and closed a few times before he crumpled to the ground, his head rolling under the console.

Finn smiled at Mila, her shoulders heaving and eyes wild. Her hoodie had a basketball-sized hole in the front, showing her taut belly covered in silver chainmail. She was sweating, her hair was coming out of its ponytail in all directions, and her makeup was smeared around her eyes, but she was the most beautiful creature he had ever seen.

Finn mustered every last scrap of strength and grit he had and lurched to his feet, scooping Mila up in his arms and diving through the door he had opened earlier. Penny was right on his heels and slapped the red button beside the center chair. The small door slid shut, and they rocketed away from the ship as the escape pod's thrusters went to full burn.

Finn looked through the small window and saw his mistreated companion, the *Anthem*, completely covered in small bubbles. As he watched, the bubbles began to expand as the ship went higher and higher. In one sudden move, they all contracted.

The *Anthem* disappeared in a haze of red mist, then the sky lit up with fire.

CHAPTER TWENTY-SIX

Mila reclined in the corner of the couch in her customary lounging clothes: black tights and a baggy t-shirt. *Star Wars: A New Hope* was playing on the TV, but she wasn't watching. She knew all the lines anyway. Instead, she watched Finn and Penny watching it, and smiled. They were enthralled, to say the least. Penny hadn't taken a bite of popcorn in the last five minutes, which might have been a record for her.

The *Anthem* had been destroyed in the early hours of Saturday, and after contacting Hermin with one of his cards, he had transported them back to Mila's condo. Danica had been waiting for them, her medical bag open and ready just in case, which had turned out to be a good call. She had patched up Finn and Mila without comment, then ordered them some food and went out.

Mila, Finn, and Penny fell asleep immediately, all tangled on the couch, and slept until late Sunday morning. Finn awoke first and made them all pancakes and coffee.

They ate and joked and didn't talk about what had happened over the last few days.

Mila guessed Finn was giving her time to process the whole thing, and she appreciated that because once she slowed down, there was a lot to think about.

That night, they'd finally sat down and talked.

Mila understood that she could never go back to the way things were before Finn and Penny showed up at the Kum & Go. That would always be the moment she would think of as dividing Before and After. Before she knew about magic, and after. Before she believed in dragons, and after. Before she understood just how small the world was, how many lives were at stake, how many others there were out there, and after.

And maybe one day, it would be the time before love...

But she knew for *sure* that it was the time before she understood what family was, and after. Finn and Penny had put their lives on the line for her and asked nothing in return. That was what family did, and it was something she had forgotten as life became more hectic, and friends fell to the wayside.

She called her mom that night and talked with her for over an hour, just to see how she was doing. It was nice.

Monday morning, she had gone into work and told them that she was taking a year of sabbatical. They put up a fuss, but in the end, she got her way and told them she would still be around if anything important came up. She wasn't planning on going anywhere in particular, but she had a feeling that she would be traveling quite a bit with Finn around.

When she went into her office, she found a note from

Jeff, this time written in English. He said that things had changed, and he begged her to not come looking for him. He believed in what the Dark Star was trying to achieve—a nation for Magicals.

She wondered if he had been coerced to write it, but she guessed she would find out eventually.

That was the main part of her talk with Penny and Finn: what to do about the Dark Star. In the end, they didn't know what to do, only that something had to be done.

Together, they decided it was a problem for a later time. Now was the time to relax and recuperate...and what better way to do that than sitting on the couch watching a movie marathon while eating their favorite junk food?

"Oh, man." Finn pointed at the screen.

Luke was checking out his lightsaber for the first time.

"I *really* want one of those," the dwarf gushed.

Mila chuckled. "*Everyone* wants one of those." She slipped her bare feet into his lap and smiled when he started rubbing her arch with his big thumb.

Penny slipped off the back of the couch, a fresh box of Charleston Chews in her hands, and curled up on Mila's lap. Keeping her eyes fixed on the screen, she reached into the box and handed one of the candies to Mila.

"Thanks."

Penny puffed a smoke ring from one nostril and patted Mila's leg affectionately before taking a bite of her chew.

Mila put her arm behind her head and popped the chew in her mouth. She closed her eyes, content for the first time in a long time.

Finn gently rubbed Mila's foot, careful not to use too much pressure. He had to be careful with her. He saw that she had painted her toenails matte black, and really liked the color against her light brown skin. It hinted at the edge she kept hidden from most people, but he had seen plenty of it over the last few days. She was strong and smart and capable like no other woman he had ever met. She was more dwarf than most dwarves he knew. His people were supposed to be rulers and to have the ability to rule without the intent. Mila had that in spades.

From the first moment he had seen her, he had been drawn to her. The whole time he was in the convenience store, he'd been hoping she would still be there when he left, and it turned out she had been going in to find him.

He liked to say it was fate, but maybe there was more at work than some unseen hand. Mila was like a beacon that he couldn't help but find in the dark. Like a black hole he couldn't escape from.

When he glanced at her, she had her eyes closed and a small smile on her face that warmed his core.

He would need to protect her. There was more to her than met the eye. Unlike most people, she had a purpose in the universe—she was a fulcrum that would lever the world. He was the son of the dwarf king, but she was important. Maybe together, they could make a difference.

He caught Penny looking at his hands, which were still methodically rubbing Mila's small foot. She glanced up at him and smiled, a ring of smoke drifting from her nostril.

He smiled and shrugged. She was right.

She usually was.

Get sneak peeks, exclusive giveaways, behind the scenes content, and more.
PLUS you'll be notified of special **one day only fan pricing** on new releases.

Sign up today to get free stories.

CLICK HERE

or visit: https://marthacarr.com/read-free-stories/

Hello everyone!

Thank you so much for reading this story, and if you are reading these notes, then a double thank you for taking the time.

This book was made possible by my favorite two things in the entire universe; a funny idea between friends, and people that are willing to give you a chance.

The funny idea came from a discussion between me and Martha about dwarves, and what they would be like in an urban fantasy setting. The idea of the short, stocky, bearded grumps we have all come to know and love felt a little ordinary for the universe Martha had created with Maggie Parker, so we wanted to do something different. I don't remember which one of us thought of it first, but we asked ourselves "What if dwarves were really tall and handsome? And the rest of the magicals didn't really like them because they were a bunch of bastards, so they just made up the whole short and ugly thing to piss them off?"

It was a funny thought experiment, but the idea stuck

in our heads. We started talking about what kinds of things he would like and do. We decided that John Wayne would become one of his heroes, and he would love to do weird things like melt Charleston Chews in his coffee, and not be able to get drunk without really strapping one on. The idea grew and grew, and we knew he had a story to tell, but he wouldn't be alone. He needed a partner. A Chewbacca to his Han.

And Penny, the blue dragon was born.

We liked the idea of a "pet" that was smarter than its owner. She was the sensible one. The snarky one. And just like a tall dwarf, we liked the idea of a small dragon.

There was just one person more needed. The one that would be able to tell Finn and Penny's story from our perspective. Mila Winters. She's smart, she's tough, and she's adaptable. And like all good heroines she has some secrets of her own to grow into.

So, now we had a cast of good strong characters. All that was left was telling their story. A good long tale that would take us from the depths of space to the couch in Mila's condo and everywhere in between. It's a good tale that you, dear reader, have just begun, and I hope you are willing to take that long journey with us.

Now for the second part; someone willing to give you a chance.

Martha and I have become friends over the years, and it all started with a late night talk at a book conference in London. I hadn't even finished my first book at the time, and didn't really know anyone at the conference, but I happened to sit down next to Martha. Best seat choice ever!

As you may know, most authors are odd at best, and me and Martha are no exception to that. We chatted a little, but we didn't know each other at all and, at first, we struggled to find common ground.

Then an angel in a black server's uniform stepped in and changed everything.

Martha, to the server: "I'll have a Prosecco."

The young, and obviously not thinking, server: "We have skinny Prosecco…" he said, with a raised eyebrow.

I thought I had seen a withering glance before, but I realized I had never seen a *real* withering glance until that very moment. Let me just say, Martha has the best one. Academy Award level wither. "How about just a Prosecco?"

The server turned red and skittered away to get her a fully-leaded Prosecco.

Me and Martha looked at one another and burst out laughing.

From that moment on we became good friends. She mentored me when I was down, and we've had conversations about everything from writing to our place in this crazy universe we all live in. She's taught me to believe in my abilities, and trust in the process.

I can't possibly repay her for her wisdom and guidance, but more than that I can't thank her enough for believing in me.

I've never met a more *real* person in my entire life.

So, I don't look at this book, and what we've created, as a business deal… it's just a continuation, an evolution, of a friendship that will last for the rest of our lives.

Thank you, dear reader, and thank you Martha.

Charley Case
Boise Idaho,
October 2019

Want to connect with me? <u>Follow me on Facebook</u> or <u>join my Facebook group</u>.

And the Universe expands! Big Welcome to Charley Case and his new series – The Adventures of Finnegan Dragonbender in the Terranavis Universe. I saw Charley's rendition of the 'Prosecco' incident in his author notes.

Tell me, who repeats a slightly older fetching woman's drink order to her and adds the word 'skinny'? Only the young or foolish.

The other part of that story he didn't mention is that we brainstormed the idea for a jean-shorts-wearing-raccoon who can't resist the call of a Taco Bell dumpster that eventually became part of The Elemental's Magic, Book 3 in The Adventures of Maggie Parker. It was a very productive night in London.

Since then, Charley and his beautiful wife and animal vet, Kelly, have stayed at my house to attend a wedding here in Austin and Charley returned for a small author summit in my living room. It's my clever way of getting people to come to me. I see the inside of way too many airports as it is.

It's given me a chance to do a lot of hanging out with the very tall, redheaded bearded and kindhearted man and I've learned a few things. He can get himself lost in a bar that granted had a few hallways but come on. He likes Coke mixed with red wine, called kalimotxo (pronounced calimocho), which means he'll fit in here really well. He's the kind of guy that if you called him in the middle of the night and you said you were in trouble – even trouble of your own making – he'd hesitate for a nice long pause and then get up and come and help you out. Then remind you about it for years to come and use parts of it in a story.

Add on top that he has a really good sense of what matters in life and wants to write a really good story. Plus, he has that weird and wicked sense of humor that I really appreciate. A really good recipe for a collaborator.

Also not a bad sprinter. In writer lingo, that's what happens when two or more writers do nothing but write as fast as they can for a set amount of time. I often sprint with Charley for 30 minutes at a time with a short break in between. However, I also have more than a few books I'm juggling (the excuse part). Sooooo… when I forgot to call 'time' for a break and after 40 minutes Charley texted me, got no answer and gave up, going online briefly to see what was happening on Facebook (you should have been writing!) and saw me doing a Facebook Live reading… he laughed and joined in, saying hello.

Best part is when the alarm on my phone went off during the live reading I wondered what that was for. And, when I noticed Charley had joined in, still didn't remember. I'm telling you, this operation is big! Lots of moving parts! He's such a nice guy, he still sprints with me and I'm still the timekeeper on occasion. I think of it as spiritual timekeeping. You occasionally will get to stop when I remember to tell you, which must be what was intended. That's my story and I'm sticking with it. Glad you all are here for this new and expanding universe! More adventures to follow.

OTHER BOOKS IN THE TERRANAVIS UNIVERSE

The Adventures of Maggie Parker Series

The Witches of Pressler Street

Other books by Martha Carr

Other books by Charley Case

JOIN THE TERRANAVIS UNIVERSE FACEBOOK GROUP

FOLLOW TERRANAVIS UNIVERSE ON FACEBOOK

CONNECT WITH THE AUTHORS

Charlie Case Social

Follow me on Facebook
or
Join my Facebook group.

Martha Carr Social

Website:
http://www.marthacarr.com

Facebook:
https://www.facebook.com/groups/MarthaCarrFans/

https://www.facebook.com/terranavisuniverse/

Michael Anderle Social

Michael Anderle Social
Website:
http://www.lmbpn.com

Email List:
http://lmbpn.com/email/

Facebook
https://www.facebook.com/TheKurtherianGambitBooks/

Made in the USA
Columbia, SC
08 June 2020